THE DUKE WHO DESPISED CHRISTMAS

CHRISTMAS DUKES
BOOK ONE

SCARLETT SCOTT

The Duke Who Despised Christmas

Christmas Dukes Book 1

All rights reserved.

Copyright © 2024 by Scarlett Scott

Published by Happily Ever After Books, LLC

Edited by Grace Bradley and Lisa Hollett, Silently Correcting Your Grammar

Cover Design by EDH Professionals

This book or any portion thereof may not be reproduced or used in any manner whatsoever without the express written permission of the publisher except for the use of brief quotations in a book review.

The unauthorized reproduction or distribution of this copyrighted work is illegal. No part of this book may be scanned, uploaded, or distributed via the Internet or any other means, electronic or print, without the publisher's permission. Criminal copyright infringement, including infringement without monetary gain, is punishable by law.

This book is a work of fiction and any resemblance to persons, living or dead, or places, events, or locales, is purely coincidental. The characters are productions of the author's imagination and used fictitiously.

For more information, contact author Scarlett Scott.

https://scarlettscottauthor.com/

For my readers, with everlasting gratitude.

CHAPTER 1

DECEMBER, 1883

Something was different at Blackwell Abbey this cold, gray winter's morning. The Duke of Sedgewick couldn't quite discern what it was, however.

Quint sniffed the air, a new, unfamiliar scent invading his nostrils. It smelled...verdant and crisp, with a slight tinge of sweetness. What the devil could it be? Whatever it was, he didn't bloody well like it.

"Dunreave!" His voice echoed in the marbled great hall like the lash of a whip cracking.

The servant who acted as both his butler and valet appeared, rather in the fashion of a wraith seeping from the old stone walls. "Your Grace?"

Dunreave was tall, though not as tall as Quint, and spare of form, with a solemn air that would have been more suited to a vicar than a domestic.

"What is that scent?" Quint demanded.

"Scent?" The man's dark brows furrowed in confusion. "What scent, sir?"

He waved a gloved hand before him in irritation, indicating the air. "The smell in this damned great hall. Something has changed. What is it?"

Dunreave cleared his throat. "To the best of my knowledge, nothing has, Your Grace."

Quint ground his jaw. "The best of your knowledge isn't sufficient, Dunreave. Something has been changed. Discover what immediately, if you please."

"Yes, Your Grace."

"You know how I feel about change," he growled.

Dunreave winced. "Of course, Your Grace. I'll inquire about the scent with Mrs. Yorke at once."

The name—as unfamiliar as the smell—made Quint's eyes narrow. "Who the hell is Mrs. Yorke?"

"The new housekeeper, Your Grace."

That information gave him pause.

Quint stiffened. "I neither want, nor need, a housekeeper at Blackwell Abbey. I have no intention of entertaining visitors of any sort."

The last housekeeper hired by his mother—a Mrs. Brome, who had borne a perpetual scowl and rattled about everywhere with her nettlesome chatelaine—had been sent away several months ago, and the household had been delightfully quiet and absent of nuisances, such as an abundance of maids, ever since. The fewer people underfoot, the better. Quint didn't like people either.

"I am aware of how Your Grace feels about housekeepers," Dunreave said dutifully.

"Then why is she here?" he snapped impatiently before giving the air another sniff.

Was the scent *her*, the unwanted housekeeper, then? If so, he'd toss her out of Blackwell Abbey himself.

Dunreave looked as if he had just swallowed a fish bone and presently had it lodged in his throat. "The dowager duchess selected her for the situation, Your Grace."

Curse his mother. Why did she insist upon interfering? He had banished her from Blackwell Abbey, and yet she continued to meddle from afar.

"There is no situation, because I *don't want a bloody housekeeper*." He was shouting by the time he finished, which he regretted.

It wasn't Dunreave's fault that Quint's mother was as stubborn as a dog who had scented his favorite pig trotter hidden in the dirt and refused to surrender until he had dug it free of the earth. In this case, Quint was the pig trotter. However, he wished to remain quite miserably buried in a tomb of his own making.

Dunreave winced again, pushing his spectacles up the bridge of his nose. "I will write the dowager duchess to inform her, Your Grace."

Quint no longer had a wife, and the distinction of referring to his mother as the dowager duchess was unnecessary. A reminder of what he lost. And yet, his mother and the domestics had grown accustomed to the change when he had married Amelia.

"I'll write her myself," he snarled, the weight of guilt and the pain of grief pressing down on his chest like a boulder, omnipresent particularly at this time of year. "But this Mrs. Yates must go."

"Mrs. Yorke, Your Grace," Dunreave corrected.

Quint's lip curled. "I don't give a damn what her name is. I just want her gone forthwith."

"Of course, sir." Dunreave bowed. "I'll find Mrs. Yorke and tell her she is dismissed at once."

"Yes. Do that."

Feeling like a churl and yet helpless to stop the frustration burning through his mangled hide, Quint decided against the ride he had planned for this morning. Instead, he spun on his heel and stalked toward the drawing room, determined to find the source of the scent.

By God, if only his mother would allow him to wallow in the countryside in peace. Bad enough that she sent him an endless string of letters exhorting him to join her in London or to accompany her to country house parties or Christ knew what societal nonsense she had deemed a proper lure. This was the third housekeeper she had sent him in the span of six months.

He stopped near the broken fountain hidden in an alcove just behind the great hall when he heard a strange sound— the tinkling of water sluicing and trickling merrily down. But no, that couldn't be. The fountain was broken.

Quint stalked into the alcove, shocked to discover that the ornate, carved fish that decorated the massive fountain were indeed spitting water, just as they had been designed to do a century earlier.

He hadn't ordered the fountain's repair.

When had it been done? And without his knowledge?

Clenching his jaw, he left the alcove, following the familiar path to the drawing room. With each step, the scent grew stronger. Until he had reached the open door and made a more astonishing discovery still.

Greenery.

Everywhere.

It festooned the mantel, hung suspended over the heavy old curtains, and in two corners of the drawing room stood not one, but *two* trees, ornamented with candles and shining trinkets and baubles.

He had finally discovered the source of the scent.

Not only had someone repaired his fountain without his consent. They had also decorated his goddamn drawing room.

"Dunreave!" he roared.

JOCELINE HAD YET to meet her employer, the Duke of Sedgewick. However, she had a sinking suspicion that she was about to, if the irate hollering and stomping footfalls nearing her were any indication.

"Dunreave!"

Oh dear.

The maid at her side cowered, dropping the candles she had been carrying to the floor in a clatter.

"Mary, you may return to the kitchens to assist Mrs. Stewart," Joceline told the wide-eyed girl, saving her from the duke's impending wrath.

She had been warned that the Duke of Sedgewick was a monster—and by his own mother, no less. Joceline was prepared to face him.

"Thank you, Mrs. Yorke." Mary fled in a flurry of drab skirts.

Joceline had only sufficient time to stiffen her spine and assume the position of an infantry soldier about to take charge. And not a moment too soon.

For the Duke of Sedgewick stalked into the hall from the drawing room, a tall and imposing figure. He was dressed to go riding, a hat clasped in his leather-glove-clad hand at one side. His blue-green eyes shot irate fire at her.

He didn't look like a monster at all. Indeed, the duke was unusually handsome. His dark-gold hair was far too long for fashion, hanging about his chiseled jaw and brushing his broad shoulders. His forehead was high, his lips full, his cheekbones well-defined. His sun-bronzed skin suggested he spent a large amount of time outside, and his coat fit snugly around his powerful arms. How strange for a duke. The aristocrats Joceline had known had been soft and pale and round about their middles. They had been nothing at all like this virile, masculine man who exuded rugged power. The Duke of Sedgewick was strikingly gorgeous.

He was also glaring at her.

"Who are you?" he demanded.

Belatedly, she dipped into a curtsy, aware she had been staring. "I am Mrs. Yorke. Your Grace, I presume?"

"You presume correctly." His gaze dipped to the mess of candles scattered over the floor. "What is the meaning of this?"

Well. She couldn't cast poor Mary beneath the carriage wheels, could she?

Joceline pinned her brightest smile to her lips. "Forgive me my clumsiness, please. I will see to it that the hall is tidied at once."

The duke scowled. "Someone else shall see to it. You are dismissed, madam."

"Dismissed, Your Grace?"

"I am giving you the sack," he enunciated coldly.

Sacked? She had only just arrived three days before. And an arduous journey it had been, too, taking the 5:15 a.m. train from King's Cross in a cramped carriage. She had traveled for many hours, hopeful that her situation at Blackwell Abbey would provide some much-longed-for permanence. To say nothing of the handsome sums she had been promised by the duchess.

"Have I done something to displease Your Grace?" she asked hesitantly, wondering if it was the dropped candles that had so distressed him.

Her Grace had mentioned that her son would be exacting. That he was content to be a hermit in the wilds of the north and that he did not prefer the company of others. That he was stern and forbidding, frigid and aloof, and that she must not expect a warm reception upon her arrival.

The dowager duchess had neglected to say that he would dismiss her upon arrival, however.

"I have no need for a housekeeper," he snarled. "Or this… this…*greenery*. Have it removed before you go."

"The greenery is part of the decorations I have organized for Christmas, Your Grace," she explained.

"We don't decorate for Christmas at Blackwell Abbey, Mrs. Young."

"Mrs. Yorke," she corrected firmly, though she knew she shouldn't.

But he had already given her the sack, had he not? Her small rebellion could not cost her anything more than what she had lost.

"I beg your pardon?" he asked with deadly menace.

Were she younger, less hardened by the world, no doubt, Joceline would have flinched and wilted at the duke's impenetrable frost. But the shell around her heart was quite firm.

She held his gaze, still smiling. "My name, Your Grace. It is Mrs. Yorke."

"It hardly signifies, madam. You'll be gone before tomorrow. Dunreave will see to the arrangements taking you to Durham."

"Of course, Your Grace." She offered him another curtsy.

"Good day." He nodded and then stalked past her.

For a moment, his scent swirled in the air he had just disturbed with his cantankerous retreat. It was a pleasant scent—musky and spicy, with hints of citrus and amber— quite unlike the man who wore it.

What an absurd contrast he was. Beautiful on the outside, harsh and angry on the inside. She sighed heavily as his footsteps faded down the hall, echoing in the grim silence that she had noted upon her arrival at Blackwell Abbey three days before and which made sense now that she had finally met the master of the estate.

At least she had yet to make herself at home in the plain, chilly housekeeper's room she had been given. Her valise was still mostly packed. But there was the matter of her incredibly brief tenure here, and no personal character from the duke to be sure, not after he had so rudely dismissed her.

Frowning, she bent to retrieve the fallen candles, placing them carefully in the apron she had donned to help Mary and the footman, Peter, with the Christmas decorations. The day had begun bright with possibility. She had made use of the holly hedges in the garden, which were quite overgrown and in need of a sound trimming anyway. And then there had been some fir boughs which had been added. How pleased she had been with the overall effect. The trees had been cut from a wooded area out of sight of the manor house and hauled on a wagon. With Christmas approaching, she had been eager to make Blackwell Abbey festive and welcoming as the dowager duchess had requested of her.

But she had been quite wrong in believing her efforts would be appreciated by the duke. It was not the first disappointment in her life, and she knew without question that it wouldn't be the last.

If only the dowager had been firmer in her warning. Joceline would never have traveled so far, uprooting her life in London, lured by the promise of many more pounds per annum than she had previously earned. Now, she would have to somehow find the funds to return, secure lodging, and start anew.

Dread curdled her stomach as she picked up the last fallen candle and stood, apron full of decorations she'd intended to place on the Christmas trees. But then, with sudden clarity, it occurred to her that the Duke of Sedgewick was not who had hired her as housekeeper. His mother had.

Joceline's smile returned.

With renewed determination, she moved toward the drawing room.

Her decorating was not yet complete. And if the duke thought he could be rid of her so easily, he was about to realize he was wrong.

CHAPTER 2

Quint returned from his ride sore, muddy, sodden, and cold.

Also, starving. He had ridden for longer than usual, needing the air and the chance to collect his thoughts after the clash with his unwanted housekeeper.

He brushed lingering snowflakes from his coat in the entry hall and handed it off, along with his hat, to the sole footman he employed. Only to belatedly realize the footman wasn't the same footman. He had red hair instead of brown, and he was taller than Peter.

"Who are you?" he demanded.

"Your Grace," the young man said, looking as nervous as he sounded. "I'm Joseph Poole, Your Grace."

"And where did you come from, Joseph Poole?"

Quint had a suspicion he already knew the answer.

"Mrs. Yorke sent for me, sir. On account of needing help with the Christmas trees, sir. Your Grace. Sir."

A village lad, and one unaccustomed to service. Not that it mattered if he had ever been a footman before. Quint didn't stand on ceremony. He had no guests, no expectations, save a warm, reasonably clean house and prompt meals. Enough to exist, nothing more. What did matter, however, was that *she* had hired the boy.

His eyebrows snapped together. "When did Mrs. Yorke send for you?"

"This morning, Your Grace."

This morning. By God, had the woman possessed the temerity to meddle with his domestics after he had told her to leave?

"I see." With a nod to the footman, Quint strode into the great hall.

"Dunreave!" he hollered.

The strange scent was still lingering in the air. The vibrant aroma of freshly cut holly boughs. Only, it was stronger. Disbelief coursing through his veins, Quint stormed toward the drawing room. Gas lamps blazed within. And somehow, impossibly, there was even more greenery. It was everywhere.

"Dunreave!"

Where was the blasted man? More importantly, where was the bloody housekeeper? He had told her to remove the greenery, not to adorn the drawing room with more of it.

Frantic footfalls sounded just before a harried-looking Dunreave arrived, out of breath, his face grim. "Yes, Your Grace?"

"What is the meaning of this?" Quint demanded.

Dunreave winced. "I warned her not to continue with her decorating. I told her that you would be terribly displeased."

"Displeased doesn't *begin* to describe what I'm feeling at the moment." He flexed his gloved hands at his sides, boiling with impotent fury, the scarred skin on his fingers tingling. "Why would she decorate the drawing room before she left for the train station? I should think that packing her valise would have proven a better use of her time."

Dunreave cleared his throat. "I'm afraid Mrs. Yorke refused to go to the train station as you requested. She insisted that she remain."

Quint thought it possible that his head might explode. He might have known that the cunning baggage wouldn't have obeyed him. She had been far too bold. Bolder than a housekeeper ought to be. And far more beautiful than any domestic he'd ever seen. But that hardly signified.

"After I sacked her?" he demanded.

"Unfortunately, yes, Your Grace."

"Why?" he growled, annoyed.

His body's instinctive reaction to the news that she was still beneath his roof was a hated reminder that there remained certain portions of his anatomy that had not been ruined by flames.

Dunreave grimaced. "She said that since she is in the employ of the dowager duchess and not you, Your Grace cannot dismiss her from her post."

"The devil she did."

Her daring was beyond the limitations of reason. He should have her tossed out of Blackwell Abbey on her rump.

"Where is she?" he asked, taking another sweeping inventory of the drawing room.

"In the housekeeper's room, the last I checked, Your Grace."

If he were a different man, a kinder man, a softer man, a man who had not tried to pull his wife from a burning building and failed, he might have found the decorations pleasant and inviting. Had his life progressed as it should have done, he would have a child by now. Perhaps even another on the way. He and his family would have gathered around those trees. Presents would have been laid beneath them.

But he was not a different man.

And he had no family.

So he left the drawing room without another word, intent upon finding the housekeeper. He would carry her out of his house over his shoulder if necessary. All he wanted was for her to go.

JOCELINE WAS INSPECTING the dishes for cracks when the heavy, booted feet of the duke pounded toward her.

Mary, poor skittish girl that she was, made a squeak of fright when he appeared at the threshold of the housekeeper's room, thunderclouds in his harsh stare and icy fury in his clenched jaw.

"You," he said to the maid, his voice clipped and steely as his eyes. "Go."

Mary didn't hesitate in fleeing. She rushed from the chamber with such haste she nearly tripped over her hems, forgetting to curtsy, mumbling something unintelligible.

Joceline suppressed a sigh and faced the Duke of Sedgewick alone for the second time that day. If his countenance was any indication, he was even more displeased with her than he had been on the previous occasion.

"Your Grace." She greeted him with as much kindness as she could summon, dipping in deference as she smiled with false cheer.

The duke did not return her smile. "Why are you still here, madam?"

"Because Her Grace deemed me suitable to fulfill the role of housekeeper here at Blackwell Abbey."

"Yes, but Her Grace is not the owner of Blackwell Abbey, and she had no right to offer you the situation," he bit out. "I neither want nor need a housekeeper. Particularly not one who is defiant and refuses to listen to the orders given her."

As he ventured nearer, Joceline once again caught his scent, mingling with the fresh earthiness of the outdoors from his ride. His long hair was damp, the ends curling. He still wore his mud-splattered riding boots. A sizzle of unexpected awareness coursed through her despite herself. There was something about the Duke of Sedgewick that was deeply compelling, regardless of his truculent disposition.

But she couldn't concern herself with that. She was a servant in his household—and an unwanted one at that. She had to do battle with him, not swoon over his handsome looks.

"I understand that you believe you don't require a housekeeper, Your Grace," she began in soothing tones before he interrupted her.

"It is not a matter of belief, Mrs. Young. It is a matter of fact."

"Mrs. Yorke," she reminded him, understanding why the dowager duchess had chosen her to fill the lofty position of housekeeper, and at a tremendously large sum per annum, too. "And I am afraid that I would beg to differ, Your Grace."

He had stopped before her, emanating a wintry menace that she had no doubt had cowed every poor housekeeper who had preceded her. "Oh? Is that so, madam?"

His voice held a deceptive calm, rather reminiscent of a serpent about to strike. But she refused to be intimidated. He may be a duke, but he was a duke who was sorely in need of some aid at his ailing estate. His mother had known it. She had warned Joceline of the challenge that would be awaiting her here in the north.

"My son has exiled himself, Mrs. Yorke," the dowager had said. "It is quite as if he died with his wife. He is allowing the estate to go to ruin around him. He has turned away almost all the domestics, including the excellent housekeepers I sent him over the last few

months, and I quite fear what will happen in the absence of a suitable domestic's firm guidance over the household."

Joceline hadn't been concerned with the duke's past at the time. Rather, she had been compelled to accept the situation because of the promised one hundred pounds per annum should she stay the whole year, a fortune compared to the modest fifty pounds she had been earning previously. But more than that, the duchess had promised her an additional fifty pounds if she was able to keep Blackwell Abbey decorated for Christmas, as Her Grace intended to visit her son for the festive season.

Joceline needed this post. Needed the one hundred pounds and the fifty pounds besides. Her younger brother and sisters made use of every shilling she could send back to them and Mama, now that Papa was gone. Many others depended upon her. Here, at last, was her chance to earn funds to keep a roof over her siblings' heads and enough food in their bellies.

So she kept her face a mask of polite civility and held the duke's stare. "That is so, Your Grace. Your household is, to be perfectly candid, in a state of ruin. The number of domestics in your employ is woefully insufficient for a manor house of this size. The kitchen maid is cavorting with one of the grooms. Your dishes are cracked and chipped and in need of repair. There is a mouse infestation that needs to be dealt with, your preserve stores are empty, and your cook is tippling the sherry. To say nothing of the carpets that need to be taken up and beaten, the abundant dust that is covering nearly every surface, the loose floorboards on the servants' stair, and the broken chandelier in the dining room."

She finished her impassioned speech and was greeted with cold silence and the duke's impassive countenance. His blue-green gaze remained glacial. He was so stern, so austere. So despicably handsome, even in his cruel indifference.

He quite took her breath, the wretched man.

And then his deep voice rumbled, cutting through the calm.

"With such a dire opinion of my household, madam, I can only wonder at your choice to festoon my drawing room with Christmas trees and gewgaws and holly branches instead of correcting any of the inadequacies you have so helpfully catalogued."

"Her Grace professed her desire that Blackwell Abbey be decorated for the Christmas season," she defended. "As Her Grace intends to be present for Yuletide, I was merely making an effort to do her bidding whilst attending to the rest."

His eyes narrowed. "Present for Yuletide? I issued no such invitation to my mother."

She forced a tight smile. "I am afraid that is an issue Your Grace will need to address with Her Grace."

"I begin to think you are colluding with my mother, madam."

Joceline narrowly avoided gritting her teeth—the man was infuriating. "I can assure you that I am not conspiring in any fashion. I am attempting to do the job I was hired for."

"At my home."

"At Your Grace's home," she agreed.

"By someone other than myself," he continued with deceptive calm.

"By Her Grace."

"Then you agree that you are trespassing."

She gaped at him. "I agree to no such thing, Your Grace."

"Whether you concur is immaterial. You cannot argue against plain fact, madam. You are here, in a place where you are not wanted, performing tasks I have not given you leave to perform, and at the behest of someone who is not the owner of this estate. You are, therefore, trespassing. I ought to send for the constable and have you thrown into jail for your temerity."

The breath fled her lungs at his cool statement. But then she inhaled, telling herself he wasn't serious about such a threat. That he couldn't be. That she had done nothing wrong.

"If you truly think to have me arrested for the crime of decorating your drawing room with Christmas greenery, then I suppose you must," she told him. "Otherwise, I do hope Your Grace will leave me to my work. There are a great deal more dishes to be inspected for damage and only so many hours in the day."

She kept her tone as sweet as honey, maintaining her poise and calm through the sheer miracle of determination and necessity.

His jaw worked, and she couldn't tell if he was holding back words or if he was grinding his molars. "I don't want you here."

Joceline continued to smile sunnily at him. "Do you like dust, mouse droppings, chipped plates, and a house in disrepair?"

"The fountain in the alcove behind the great hall," he growled. "Was that you?"

Ah, he had noticed her little triumph. No doubt, it displeased him greatly, just as everything else she had done in her short tenure here.

"It was Joseph Poole, Your Grace. He is a new footman I have taken the liberty of hiring."

"Footmen are not a part of the housekeeper's domain."

"I am aware. However, poor Mr. Dunreave is already burdened with far too many tasks, and since he was reluctant to hire new servants for fear of Your Grace's displeasure, I took on the task myself."

Fortunately, she had found the industrious Joseph Poole

in the village, along with a handful of others who were willing to work at Blackwell Abbey. Joseph had quite handily repaired the broken fountain.

The duke's lip curled. "Dunreave is a wise and loyal man."

"Yes, Your Grace. On that, we are in complete accord."

"I want you gone tomorrow. Leave on the first train that returns to London. If my mother wishes for you to be a housekeeper so badly, then you may be hers. Good day, Mrs. Yorke."

Without waiting for her response, the Duke of Sedgewick spun on his heel and stalked from the room. She watched his tall, stately figure retreating, belatedly realizing he had finally called her by the correct name.

CHAPTER 3

Quint glared at his reflection in the mirror as Dunreave smoothed a razor over his jaw. He had spent the previous evening stewing over his confrontation with Mrs. Yorke, her observations about his household taunting him, along with the reminder of how comely she was. How ripe her lips had been, stretched into a polite smile that no amount of surliness on his part had shaken. She possessed a mouth that was infinitely kissable, and he resented his own weakness for noticing.

He hadn't been aware of a woman in a physical sense in some time. Not since Amelia's death. First, he had been too badly injured by grief and the burns he had suffered in the fire to give a damn. Later, he had healed physically—his ravaged skin no longer blistering and oozing, but hideously scarred—and yet, the grief had remained.

So, too, the guilt, the nightmares, the pain of knowing he might have saved her, had he only been a few minutes sooner. He had buried himself alongside her in the graveyard at Sedgewick Hall, and then he had traveled north, to one of his lesser holdings here at Blackwell Abbey, bringing only a small contingent of domestics with him, remaining far from every reminder of Amelia and the terrible fire that had claimed her and their unborn babe that hated December.

Why now, of all times, should he be reminded that he was indeed a flesh-and-blood male, that his disfigured body still had needs? He hated himself for the unwanted yearning that had begun to boil in his blood from the moment he had first seen his raven-haired housekeeper. And he despised her for being so lovely, so filled with a surfeit of cheer, for intruding upon the place where he had walled himself away in his misery, for knowing more about Blackwell Abbey in a handful of days than he did.

For making him want her.

He had to distract himself.

"Dunreave?"

The razor sliced into his flesh.

He hissed in pain, watching in the mirror as the shaving soap's foam turned red.

"Forgive me, Your Grace!" Dunreave cried. "I can be so clumsy sometimes."

The fault was Quint's. Not just for talking whilst the sometimes butler, sometimes valet shaved him. But for requiring Dunreave to play so many roles in his household.

Mrs. Yorke's tart words came back to him.

Poor Mr. Dunreave is already burdened with far too many tasks.

He cleared his throat, reaching for a handkerchief and pressing it to the shallow wound. "You needn't apologize, Dunreave. The fault is mine for speaking when I know you need a steady hand."

"I am so sorry, Your Grace," Dunreave fretted. "I hope my carelessness won't cause a scar."

Quint chuckled grimly. "One more scar won't cause a bit of a difference. Don't fret."

His manservant went ashen. "Forgive me, sir. I didn't mean to suggest—"

Quint held up a hand as he interrupted. "I know you didn't, Dunreave."

No one else had seen the extent of Quint's scars except for the physician who had attended him. Dunreave had nursed Quint through his many weeks of recuperation, barring Quint's mother from the sickroom at his request. By the time he had healed sufficiently to receive his mother, he had been able to don a shirt and coat and the gloves that shielded the evidence of his failure from the prying eyes of the world.

He intended to keep it that way.

He dabbed at the small nick in his jaw some more. The blood had already slowed.

"Allow me, Your Grace," Dunreave said. "I'll finish my task so that you can carry on with your day."

But suddenly, Quint was no longer interested in completing his shave. Instead, the questions that had begun festering within him ever since his clash with Mrs. Yorke bubbled up to the surface like water roiling in a pot.

"Leave it," he said. "My whiskers scarcely show anyhow. I have a question for you, Dunreave."

"Yes, Your Grace?" The manservant was grim, almost as if he expected to be sacked.

Was Quint that much of a tyrant? Strange how he hadn't noticed the fear in Dunreave's bearing before.

"Are you overburdened with tasks?" he asked and then almost winced at how much he sounded like that blasted woman.

Mrs. Yorke.

That stubborn, capable, determined, beautiful housekeeper who had invaded his home and filled his drawing room with holly and dared to defy him.

"I am happy to serve Your Grace in whatever capacity I may," Dunreave said with politic care.

Which meant that he was, indeed, overburdened in his role as butler and valet and whatever else Quint required of him in the moment.

He dipped a cloth into the bowl of water Dunreave had drawn and laid before him with the shaving implements, then began to rinse the remainder of the shaving soap from his face. "Would it aid you if I were to hire a valet to attend me?"

"I would never presume to ask Your Grace to do so."

A telling response.

"But would it help you, Dunreave?" he pressed, rinsing the last of the lather from his jaw and trying not to wince as the small cut on his jaw stung. "That is what I asked."

"Yes, Your Grace. It would."

He finished his task and turned to his valet. "Is there a rodent problem here at Blackwell Abbey?"

A flush tinged Dunreave's cheekbones. "Your Grace should not contend with such matters."

"*Is* there one?"

"There is."

Damn Mrs. Yorke for being correct.

"And are there loose boards on the servants' stair?" he asked next, thinking of his unwanted housekeeper's list of faults she had already found with Blackwell Abbey.

"Peter is meant to repair them," Dunreave said. "There are so few of us that we know where to step to avoid injury."

Dear God. She had been right about that as well. What else was she right about?

"Does Cook tipple the sherry?"

Dunreave cleared his throat, looking distinctly uncomfortable and giving Quint his answer. "I'm certain I could not say whether Mrs. Steward does so, Your Grace."

Grimacing, he passed a hand along his jaw. "Is Mrs. Yorke still here?"

He was reasonably certain that the stubborn woman was. That—just like the previous day—she had flouted his orders.

"I believe that she is, Your Grace. When last I saw her, she was instructing the new scullery maid on the most efficient means of scouring a pot."

Of course she was. Had he doubted it?

"Thank you, Dunreave. Will you tell Mrs. Yorke that I require a word with her in my study in half an hour's time?"

"Yes, Your Grace."

He intended to have a meeting with the meddlesome housekeeper. If she was to remain here at Blackwell Abbey, they needed to set some rules.

JOCELINE ARRIVED at the duke's study at the prescribed hour, prepared to go to war.

He was standing at the window as she entered, a tall, imposing figure presiding over his kingdom, clad in severe black trousers and coat, the same leather gloves he had been wearing the day before covering his hands. She took note because they were clasped behind his back in an indolent pose. Yesterday, she had assumed the gloves had been for riding. Today, however, he did not look as if he were dressed to take one of his horses out across the chilly park.

"You requested an interview with me, Your Grace?" she asked into the stillness when he refused to turn and acknowledge her arrival, despite having bid her to enter when she had knocked at the closed door.

He cast a glance over his shoulder, briefly meeting her gaze before resuming his vigil at the window. "Yes, I did, Mrs. Yorke. Close the door, if you please."

His voice was not nearly as sharp or cold as it had been the day before when he had confronted her belowstairs. She had expected glacial fury at her refusal to obey his demand that she leave Blackwell Abbey in the morning. She hadn't expected a polite request for a word with her, however.

She scarcely knew what to expect from him, but she turned and did his bidding, making certain the door to his study was fully closed. When she spun about, it was to find the full, brilliant intensity of his gaze on her.

"Your Grace." Joceline dipped into a curtsy, the chatelaine at her waist clinking merrily as she did so.

For a brief moment, his eyes dipped, following the sound, but then his stare was once more burning into hers. "I have been speaking with Dunreave this morning, Mrs. Yorke, and it would seem that some of your observations about Blackwell Abbey were indeed quite astute."

He could have pushed her flat onto her bottom with nothing more than a feather, so complete was her astonishment. She had expected another firm harangue. Perhaps a renewed threat to have her sent to the nearest jail. Certainly, she had not anticipated an acknowledgment that she had been correct in her assessment of his estate.

"You have?" she squeaked, cursing herself for the surprise that made her voice unnaturally high.

He inclined his head in a regal manner. "I have."

He wasn't intending to sack her then, was he?

"I am relieved to hear it," she managed politely. "Does this mean that you are no longer as reluctant to accept my presence?"

His lips twitched, but his visage remained unsmiling. "You may stay for now, madam."

Relief swept over her. "Thank you, Your Grace."

"Don't thank me," he clipped. "I do not like mice, Mrs.

Yorke. You will remain long enough to set my household in order, and then you will return to London."

Joceline couldn't contain her smile. "Of course, Your Grace."

He scowled. "Are you always so annoyingly full of cheer, madam?"

A hysterical laugh threatened to burst forth. She tamped it down with all the restraint she possessed. If only he knew how difficult her life had been thus far and how much struggle she had endured. He never would have asked such a question of her.

But the Duke of Sedgewick didn't know her. It wasn't his place to know her. She was but a servant in his household, just as she had been in others prior to his. Her past was immaterial to him, and lest she confuse his generosity for anything else, she must not forget that his sole reason for relenting and allowing her to remain was his *dislike of mice*.

"I can assure Your Grace that it has never been my intention to annoy you," she said, her smile fading. "Pleasing you is my sole desire."

She hadn't intended for her words to have such a carnal undertone, but the moment they were uttered, something in the room shifted. The duke's blue-green gaze slid once more, this time to her lips rather than to her chatelaine. Deep within her, a yearning that she had long since learned to quell surged forth before she could stop it. She was not meant to be a woman of emotion, base or otherwise. She had been born to be a woman of duty and tasks, with work-roughened hands. Her sole occupation was in the smooth running of a household. Not passion. Not longing. Never such dangerous, decadent fancies.

"Is it?" he asked thoughtfully, moving toward her in a slow, measured saunter, away from the window.

He reached her, stopping to loom over Joceline, the scent

of him filling her lungs, and she caught herself inhaling deeply to gather more of it. His gloved fingertips were on his jaw, stroking. And that was when she noticed the cut at this proximity, marring the sleek architecture of his beautiful face. The golden whiskers glinting in the sunlight only on one half of his face. A shaving injury, then.

Her cheeks went hot at the realization, so intimate. It wasn't her place to think of him shaving. It wasn't her place to think of him at all. Certainly not in the way a woman thinks about a man.

"It is, Your Grace," she said, cursing herself for the breathlessness in her voice.

This was unlike her, to be affected by her employer. But then, she had never had an employer as dangerously mesmerizing as the Duke of Sedgewick.

He leaned down, shocking her. For one wild moment, she thought he might do something untoward. That he might set his sculpted, sullen lips to hers. But then he spoke with quiet warning into her ear.

"If you truly wish to please me, Mrs. Yorke, then you will remove the Christmas greenery and trees from my damned drawing room."

She stepped back from him, jolted, frightened by her body's reaction to his, by the ache that blossomed deep in her belly and sank lower to a more forbidden place. All from his scent and his nearness and the silken velvet of his voice giving her more churlish commands.

"Her Grace requested the decorations, if you will recall," she reminded him firmly, refusing to allow him to see how badly he had discomfited her.

Likely, the duke would be pleased to know it. She had no wish to be the source of his amusement.

He clenched his jaw, once more unyielding. "And if you will recall, I am allowing you to remain because you have shown yourself to be a reasonably capable housekeeper. Do not make me rethink my leniency, madam."

They stared at each other, awareness crackling between them like thunder in a summer storm. She did not think she mistook the raw, masculine interest in his gaze. It did not shock her that a duke would take carnal interest in his housekeeper; aristocrats often dallied with their domestics. It was frowned upon, but all too commonly done. What astonished her, however, was that this rigid, icy, forbidding man was attracted to anyone at all, let alone *her*.

She would not allow him to know just how vulnerable she was to his interest. A respectable housekeeper who wished to remain respectable must, at all times, forget that she was a woman of flesh and bone. Forget that she had needs and wants. Her lot was to be as emotionless and useful as a piece of furniture adorning a room. Serviceable. Sturdy. Necessary. But an object incapable of thought or feeling.

"Very well, Your Grace," she relented. "I will see to it that the Christmas greenery and trees are removed from the drawing room. Joseph and Peter are laying out mouse poison and traps for the rodent problem at this moment, but I will divert them forthwith to the task of removing all the decorations. I should think it will take them the remainder of the day to have it all taken away, and then they will need to find a place where they can take the trees and garlands, along with a proper cart to do so. The cart they used previously has a broken axle. I am sure it will take no more than two days at the most to have all the decorations removed before they can return to the effort of curbing the mice."

The consternation on his arrogant face might have been amusing were her circumstances not so very dire. She was exaggerating, of course. Only Joseph was setting mouse traps at the moment. And the removal of the decorations wouldn't take nearly as long as she had estimated. However, the Duke of Sedgewick didn't need to know that.

"Leave it for now, Mrs. Yorke." His voice was cold and stern, a distinct contrast to the fires of interest smoldering in his eyes when he looked at her. "I want the rodents dealt with first. The rest can wait a day or two."

Victory was hers. For this interview, at least. She was to have a reprieve from her sacking, and he would allow her to keep her elaborate, painstaking Christmas decorations in place. In the meantime, she would simply have to craft more clever excuses why the greenery couldn't be taken away quite yet.

Joceline tamped down a smile, knowing that she didn't dare show him just how pleased she was. Perhaps there was still hope she could crack his hardened shell. The dowager duchess would be happy to see that Joceline had at least made some progress. Unlike the previous housekeepers the dowager duchess had sent to Blackwell Abbey, Joceline had not been unceremoniously deposited back at the train station within her first few days.

"That is most generous of you, Your Grace," she said demurely. "Thank you."

"As soon as the mice are dealt with, I expect the holly and trees to be gone," he reminded her sternly.

"Would Her Grace not wish to enjoy the decorations during her stay at Blackwell Abbey?" she inquired lightly, knowing she was pushing him and yet unable to keep quiet.

The fifty pounds the dowager Duchess of Sedgewick had promised Joceline was a potent lure indeed. Her family would needed those funds desperately.

"Her Grace is not visiting Blackwell Abbey," the duke snapped with finality. "As I've told you, I've not extended an invitation."

"Of course, Your Grace," she acceded hastily, content to leave the matter for now.

She had already pressed him enough, and she didn't dare to push him any further at the moment. There was always tomorrow.

"Thank you, Mrs. Yorke," he said curtly. "That will be all."

She had been dismissed.

Joceline dipped into a curtsy. "Thank you, Your Grace. Good day."

He inclined his head, that unusual blue-green stare of his far too intent. With nothing more to say, she fled to the safety of the endless list of duties awaiting her.

CHAPTER 4

Unless he was mistaken, the scent of greenery and fir was even more pronounced this morning as Quint descended the staircase in search of his breakfast. He reached the last step and frowned, sniffing the air. There was the smell of soap and freshly scrubbed floors, which was decidedly new—and appreciated, now that he thought upon it. But no mistaking it. There was also the verdant scent of cut greens and trees, redolent and, though he would never admit it aloud, almost pleasant, reminiscent of a time when he hadn't despised Yuletide to his marrow.

What the devil had come over him?

He was about to stalk to the dining room for his customary morning coffee when some bustling about the library down the hall caught his attention. Footmen. At least four of them, entering his library. By God, had Mrs. Yorke hired even more domestics? Where had the meddlesome woman found them? He wasn't sure if he should be irritated or impressed.

Strangely, some perverse part of him was leaning toward the latter, which shocked him. He was beginning—somehow, and against his better judgment—to *like* his unwanted housekeeper. The realization almost had him tripping over his own feet as he neared the library and the source of the commotion.

As he reached the threshold, the sight that greeted him stopped Quint short.

More Christmas trees.

More holly.

And ribbons, too, and oranges and roses and apples, and sweet Christ above, was that a kissing bough hanging from the ceiling?

He goggled at the scene, taking note of the sheer abundance of decorations, before his gaze settled upon the lone feminine figure whose back was to him. She wore a gown as black as her hair, a tidy white apron looped around her waist and blanketing the front of her skirts. Her raven hair was confined in a tidy chignon at her nape. And he suddenly itched to pluck out her hairpins and sift his fingers through those inky tresses, to see if they felt as silken and smooth as they looked.

What was the matter with him? He should be outraged at this blatant disregard for his edict. And yet, he was standing here mooning over his housekeeper's hair.

"Your Grace!" Peter—thankfully a familiar face in the sea of footmen and maids busily at work—exclaimed, spying Quint amidst the flurry.

Mrs. Yorke whirled about, her customary sunny smile on her lush lips as her gaze clashed with his. "Good morning, Your Grace."

Her curtsy was faultless. She was too young, too beautiful to be a housekeeper. Where had his mother found her?

The room had come to a stop around her, a hive of bees that had been summarily stopped, the new footmen and housemaids frozen, their eyes wide. He was ever cognizant of their audience. And of the fact that she had once again defied him, to stunning effect.

"A word with you alone, Mrs. Yorke," he said with deceptive calm.

Because inside, he was a maelstrom of contrasting emotions, all of which were dangerous.

"Of course, Your Grace." Still smiling, she turned to her assemblage. "Return to your posts, if you please. I'll fetch you when I'm ready for additional assistance."

It was on the tip of Quint's tongue to tell her that she wouldn't require any more assistance, unless it meant tearing down the holly and trees and other festive nonsense that was cluttering up his library. But he remained quiet instead, venturing deeper into the room so the domestics could file out of the chamber past him.

She kept her emerald gaze carefully averted as the last of the servants retreated. Quint knew it because he couldn't wrest his own stare from her. The chatelaine at her waist draped over the apron—the trappings of her trade so plainly on display. And yet, the bold reminders that she was a domestic in his employ and forbidden to him did nothing to quell the sudden, maddening ardor coursing through him.

He was wildly attracted to her, his body feeling as if it had been awakened from a two-year-long slumber. And yet he very much could not have her. She was a Mrs. Yorke, after all, and although many housekeepers assumed the title of missus for ease, he had not inquired if she had a husband elsewhere, pining after her.

The thought had him clenching his fists at his sides and clamping down his jaw. The door clicked discreetly closed, and at last, he was alone with her. Alone in a room filled with the evidence of her insolence. He didn't know which he wanted more, to reprimand her or to take her in his arms.

But he couldn't do what he truly wished. Not with her.

So he took a deep breath, settling upon musts rather than needs. "Mrs. Yorke, would you care to explain why you have desecrated my library?"

Her hands were clasped at her waist. Dainty hands for a housekeeper, though chapped and reddened by work. He found himself oddly fascinated by those hands, wondering what they would feel like on his ruined skin. It had been so long since a woman had touched him. The memory was distant and obscure, almost like a dream he'd once had but could no longer remember.

"I would hardly call holly and fir and a few ribbons a desecration, Your Grace," she was saying with her customary cheer.

The woman could likely stand in the midst of a deluge, thunder and lightning cracking all around her, and still smile as if she were not being pelted with rains and facing imminent danger.

He itched to touch her, so he stalked to one of the twin Christmas trees that had been erected, plucking a candle from its boughs instead. "And I cannot help but to think there is no other way to view your deliberate rebelliousness. After I have given you a reprieve and deigned to allow you to stay, you decided to fill yet another room in my house with Christmastide rubbish. One can only think that you have no desire to keep your present situation."

The candle was a small weight in his gloved hand, and he couldn't say why, but he longed to touch it without the barrier of leather. To feel the pine needles on the tree, the sticky sap coating his fingertips. To *feel*, full stop.

"Or perhaps I am hoping to change your mind, Your Grace," she said, her quiet yet throaty voice sending another rush of yearning through him.

Damn his unruly body. Since when had he been so incapable of controlling his base urges?

He gave her a tight smile laden with menace. "An impossible feat, madam. I have no intention of celebrating Christmas. No number of trees and trinkets will alter that."

"One may decorate and yet still decline to celebrate," she suggested. "The decorations are for your mother. I have been arranging the rooms as she asked of me when she hired me to be your housekeeper."

"I've already told you that I neither want, nor need, a housekeeper and that, above all else, I have no wish for Blackwell Abbey to be trussed up like a Michaelmas goose. You have overstepped your bounds."

"Do you find the decorations unpleasant?" she asked.

"It doesn't matter."

"Perhaps it does. Why are you so vehemently opposed to Christmas? Is it the same reason you wear gloves?"

Quint felt as if all the blood had drained from him. These were not subjects he wished to discuss. Not with her, not with anyone. He was as he was, and that was simply that. Heaven knew what it had cost him to get to where he was. To be alive when he had failed Amelia and she was forever lost to him, ever since that fateful morning three weeks before Christmas. Yuletide had been hateful without her, each day that passed a reminder of what he would never have.

"You ask questions you haven't the right to ask, Mrs. Yorke," he told her coolly. "Do not mistake my generosity for weakness."

"Forgive me, Your Grace. I only seek to understand you."

"Understanding me is not a part of your duties."

Somehow, they had come together. He wasn't sure which of them had moved first. Perhaps they both had. But now, they were standing dangerously near, the scent of holly and fir and something else that was distinctly her surrounding them. It was floral and light, like a spring garden filled with sweet-smelling blooms.

THE DUKE WHO DESPISED CHRISTMAS

"Pleasing you is, however," she countered softly. "And to please you, Your Grace, I must also understand you. The two are inextricably intertwined."

When she spoke of pleasing him, God help him, he wasn't thinking about the cleanliness of his floors, the organization of his domestics, or the absence of mice from his kitchens. He was thinking about something else entirely. Something that was sinful, shameful, and wrong. That involved lifting her onto the nearest table, hauling her skirts to her waist, and sliding deep inside her.

"There is only one way you can please me," he bit out before he could stop himself, frustrated, furious, and vexed to the point of sheer madness.

Her dark eyebrows winged upward, her full lips parting. And to his everlasting shame, he was imagining those lips on him, gliding over his scarred skin, wrapping around his cock, which had suddenly roared to life and was straining against the placket of his trousers.

"How, Your Grace?" she asked, her soft voice a Siren's lure in itself.

Like the rest of her, that husky contralto was far too lovely not to be a temptation.

He swallowed hard, willing his erection to abate. "By doing what I've required of you. Remove the decorations you have so willfully hung all over my home."

"Do you find fault with my decorating?" she had the temerity to ask.

"The mice, madam," he reminded her. "I allowed you to stay because you promised to take care of the mouse infestation. Yesterday, you claimed the footmen were otherwise occupied with setting traps and laying poison bait belowstairs. And yet today, rather than removing the decorations from the drawing room, you have added additional greenery and trees to my library. That tells me that you are a liar. How am I to keep you in my employ when you have deceived me? What is next, I wonder? Will you be filching the family silver?"

She went pale at his question. "I am not a thief, Your Grace. I am merely a servant in your household, attempting to perform the duties Her Grace the dowager duchess expects of me."

He hated himself for his weakness where Mrs. Yorke was concerned. Hated himself for desiring a woman at all, let alone a servant. It was wrong. And yet, she was as intoxicating as an elixir. He wanted her.

Desperately.

He couldn't have her.

Quint gripped the candle in an iron fist, so tightly that it was a miracle the wax didn't snap in two. "And as I have already informed you, Her Grace is not the master of Blackwell Abbey. I am, and you have lied to me repeatedly over the few short days you have been here. You have run roughshod over my house and my wishes. You have hired servants I do not want and filled my rooms with Christmas bric-a-brac. I ought to turn you out at once without a character and make you walk to the train station on foot."

Yes, he ought to do that. But he didn't have it in him. And he wanted her here. Beneath his roof. Even if it meant enduring more holly boughs and fir trees. The realization had him rubbing the back of his neck with his free hand. He had been one man before the fire and a new man after. But now, standing in perilous proximity to his gorgeous housekeeper, Quint was a third man.

Someone he didn't recognize.

"Please don't send me away," she begged him, those vibrant green eyes of hers searing him to his soul.

He was the beast he saw in the mirror.

"Then obey me," he snarled, before stalking from the library.

It wasn't until he had reached the dining room and his cooling breakfast that Quint realized he was still holding the bloody candle from the Christmas tree.

∽

JOCELINE INWARDLY CHASTISED herself that afternoon as she left the kitchens after making the latest preparations with Cook. In the absence of a lady of the house, she had begun presiding over the menu decisions and other matters. But it wasn't the stoning of plums for Christmas plum pudding that was the reason for her self-castigation. Rather, it was her embarrassing reaction to the Duke of Sedgewick. In itself, the way he made her feel was not just maddening, it was perplexing.

He was fractious, he was cold, and on so many occasions, he was also rude. His handsomeness could not offset his frigid personality. He was rigid and unfeeling. He had called her a liar and threatened to have her removed from his home. He had accused her of wanting to steal his silver next. At every turn, he met her attempts at cheer with grim disapproval. He snarled and growled and glowered. All the domestics in his employ feared incurring his wrath.

And more than that, he was not just her employer, but a duke. She should know better than to long for that which was beyond her reach. What had she been thinking, standing so near to Sedgewick in the library, wondering what his mouth would feel like on hers, daring to ask him questions she knew that she had no right to ask?

She sighed heavily as she neared the housekeeper's room, a joyless, dismal chamber which was dank and cold despite the plentiful fire burning in the hearth. By now, Joceline was accustomed to life in service. Any dreams she had once harbored for her future had died some time ago, along with her father.

She had set them aside in favor of helping her mother and siblings. It had not always been the way of it, of course. When she had been quite young, there had been the ever-elusive hope that she might have a London Season with her aunt, Mama's sister, one day. As the eldest child, with lovely looks, as Mama had said, Joceline had been sent away to stay with her aunt for much of her girlhood. Mama had been filled with catching sanguinity the day she had seen Joceline off to London.

That hopefulness had transformed into bleak acceptance over time. For although she had been permitted to share her cousins' governess for several years, there had been a distinct line between Joceline and her cousins. She was the poor relation being given alms through the good grace of her aunt, the baroness. Emily and Catherine, however, were the daughters of a baron. When Joceline reached the age for her debut, she had been sent back to her parents, where her father was an invalid and a growing brood of children had rendered their family quite destitute. She had gone to service shortly thereafter, having no other option but to work and send what meager funds she could save home.

She had been fortunate in her placement, working her way up from chambermaid to housekeeper within several years, thanks to her education, her polite elocution, and her dedication to her craft. At five-and-twenty, she knew that the gravest mistake anyone in service could ever make was to grow too fond of an employer or to overstep her bounds. The lines between them were invisible—and yet, as immovable as a castle wall.

This dreadful malaise, or whatever it was, that had affected her since her arrival at Blackwell Abbey, was a

THE DUKE WHO DESPISED CHRISTMAS

terrible aberration. Joceline had never been attracted to her employer before. She had never longed for him to kiss her. She had never wanted anything more than her salary, her position, and a letter of character if she moved on to another household.

And yet that morning, she had inexplicably found herself yearning for the Duke of Sedgewick. Wanting to know his secrets. Wanting his arms around her, his mouth on hers. Wanting even more.

"Foolish, foolish woman," she scolded herself beneath her breath as she crossed the threshold into her private room, closing the door at her back. "What were you thinking?"

With another sigh, she began untying her apron.

And that was when she saw him. Tall, decadently handsome, and forbiddingly austere.

Sitting on her chair as if it were the most natural place in the world for him to rest. As if he belonged there.

She gasped instinctively, startled, pressing a hand to her madly beating heart. "Your Grace."

Remembering herself, she dipped into a curtsy.

"Sit, Mrs. Yorke."

His countenance was unreadable, his voice a low rumble that sent a frisson of something dangerous down her spine. He gestured to another chair not far from his, the one where Mr. Dunreave would sit when they reviewed matters pertaining to the household.

Warily, she did as the duke commanded, seating herself primly on the edge, rather as if she were poised for flight. One never knew what to expect from the Duke of Sedgewick.

She folded her hands in her lap. "Is there something you wished to speak with me about, Your Grace?"

And if so, it was most irregular for him to come belowstairs, to her private room, rather than ringing for her. But she wisely kept that to herself.

He nodded, his stare cool and assessing. "Dunreave told me you were meeting with Cook concerning the menu. I decided to await you here. I hope you don't mind."

Where was the growling, surly man who had been so outraged over the garlands and trees in his library? He was perfectly calm. Almost even polite.

She blinked. "Of course not, Your Grace. You are more than welcome to await me here whenever it pleases you."

Drat. There it was again, that word. *Please.* It somehow took on a sensual meaning whenever she spoke it in his presence. Heat rose to her cheeks, and she hoped he wouldn't take note of her embarrassing reaction.

"I hardly think so," he said, an odd expression flashing over his handsome countenance for just a moment before it fled.

What was he saying? Surely not what her foolish mind had inferred?

"Who were you speaking to when you entered?" he asked before she could further contemplate the questions whirling in her mind.

"Myself, I'm afraid," she admitted, certain she was red as a beet by now.

She must have been wrong to think there was even a hint of sexual innuendo in what he'd said. The Duke of Sedgewick had made it brutally clear he didn't even like her and that he only tolerated her presence for his own peace of mind and on an entirely temporary basis.

To her surprise, a small smile flirted with the corners of his lips. "And do you make a good conversation partner, Mrs. Yorke?"

The effect of that tiny smile had her breath catching. If she had thought the duke handsome before, nothing could

THE DUKE WHO DESPISED CHRISTMAS

have prepared her for the Duke of Sedgewick *smiling*. He had dimples on both cheeks, a small groove that deepened just the slightest hint.

Belatedly, she realized he was staring at her, waiting for her response.

"I have often been the only conversation partner I've had, Your Grace. As such, I must admit to partiality."

"Is it a solitary life, then, that of housekeeper?"

His marked interest was most disconcerting. How astonishing to be the full recipient of not just his gaze, but his full attention as well. And not in anger either.

"I suppose it must be at times," she answered earnestly. "Unlike some of the other servants, we must carefully separate ourselves from the rest, lest they become too familiar. A maid who thinks herself friends with the housekeeper will not heed her. Most often, when I hold a conversation with anyone, it is to tell them which of their tasks must be performed next."

"How long have you been a housekeeper, Mrs. Yorke? You do seem rather young for such a weighty task."

"I have been employed as a housekeeper for these past four years, and I am five-and-twenty," she answered easily, wondering how old he was.

No more than a decade her senior, she would wager.

"Have you always been in service?" he queried next. "You are remarkably well-spoken for a servant. Forgive me my bluntness, but I couldn't help but to take note."

"I have been in service since I was sixteen, and I thank you for the compliment. I owe my education to my aunt, Baroness Rothermel. I was permitted to live with her during much of my younger years, and my cousins' governess taught me as well."

"And these cousins and this aunt of yours, where are they now? Never say they abandoned you to a life of service." He frowned, looking as if the thought displeased him.

But that was impossible, surely. He was the Duke of Sedgewick, and she was nothing more than his housekeeper. Why would he concern himself with the vagaries of her past? Why would he want to know about old hurts and betrayals and disappointments she had long since locked away deep inside her heart?

"They returned me to my family when I was of an age to make my debut," she explained, and not without some of the old bitterness returning. "My father was an invalid and unable to support my mother and siblings. Someone needed to go to work so they didn't starve. When he died, that became even more apparent."

"And so, instead of making your curtsy, you became a servant," he guessed, his expression darkening.

She forced a smile she didn't feel—dwelling on the past had never done her one whit of good, and none of it could be changed. "I did what I had to do."

"How did you begin in service?" Sedgewick asked next.

His intense regard and proximity here, in the confined space that was solely hers, heightened her awareness of him. She thought back to her first situation when she had been a green girl of sixteen. It was difficult to believe that nearly ten years had passed since she had left her siblings and Mama behind. She hadn't been able to visit often, preferring to send everything she could home to them rather than waste it on the cost of travel.

"I began as a maid of all work for a wealthy widow," she said. "I was fortunate to find an excellent situation. The character she provided me enabled me to become a chambermaid next, and then the sudden illness of a housekeeper at yet another situation allowed me to fill the role. I suppose I proved myself suited to the task."

"And these letters of character were provided to Her Grace, I presume."

"Are you interviewing me for the position of housekeeper, Your Grace?" she asked, the notion belatedly occurring to her, and not without a sharp pang of disappointment she had no right to feel.

He was not interested in *her*. Rather, he was interested in her qualifications. Her background.

He inclined his head. "I reckon I am, Mrs. Yorke. I'll admit that you vex me mightily with your propensity for flouting my authority at every turn. However, Blackwell Abbey is cleaner than I can recall ever seeing it, the household is running with an efficiency I wouldn't have thought possible, and just this morning, I enjoyed the best breakfast I've eaten in years, followed by an excellent luncheon. Although it aggrieves me to admit it, your unparalleled skill at managing my home and domestics leaves me somewhat in awe."

He was in awe of her. For her housekeeper skills, of course. Her stupid heart tripped over itself anyway.

"Thank you, Your Grace," she managed, astounded by his sudden sea change.

Naturally, it was for his own comfort. It behooved him to keep her in his service. Joceline knew she was a good housekeeper. However, she hadn't expected the arrogant Duke of Sedgewick to acknowledge her skill or be moved by it.

"Will you stay at Blackwell Abbey, then, Mrs. Yorke?" he asked, an earnestness in his tone that struck some part of her.

She had never intended to leave, but Joceline knew she needn't tell him that. Instead, she thought of the fifty pounds she could send to Mama and the children. The duchess had been firm that it was only to be hers if the Christmas decorations remained in place.

"What of the holly garlands and Christmas trees?" she ventured.

He raised a brow. "If having my drawing room and library festooned in greenery and filled with trees will keep you here, then I suppose it must stay."

Joceline couldn't contain her smile. "That is wonderful news, Your Grace. I would be pleased to remain here at Blackwell Abbey."

The duke nodded and rose to his full, impressive height. She stood as well, trying not to take note of what a dashing figure he cut and failing miserably. His dark-gold hair brushed his broad shoulders, and a hint of whiskers shaded the bold slash of his jaw.

"Is there a Mr. Yorke, madam?" he asked suddenly, startling her with both the question and the unexpected nature of it.

"No, Your Grace," she answered swiftly. "There is not."

"Are you a widow, then?"

"I've never been married, Your Grace."

He stared at her for a moment longer, and she held her breath, doing everything she could to keep from looking at his mouth or to think about what it would be like to close the distance between them and slip her arms around his neck. To rise on her toes and press her lips to his. To tug at his necktie and unbutton his shirt and reveal the muscle and man beneath his country tweed. To remove his gloves and discover what he was hiding from the world.

But she could do none of those things.

The Duke of Sedgewick simply nodded, looking unmoved, whilst she was inwardly waging a battle of epic proportions.

"Good day, Mrs. Yorke," he told her politely.

And then, he left her room just as stealthily as he had

invaded it, leaving her behind with a racing heart and the flames of longing she could not afford to fan.

CHAPTER 5

"Flowers."

Quint stared bemusedly at a vase in the great hall, which was placed upon a table he'd never seen before. He knew who was responsible for the vibrant blossoms without needing to ask. For the table as well. The only thing he didn't know was how she had managed to find the flowers in the midst of winter or where she had discovered the damned table.

"Yes, Your Grace," Dunreave said hastily. "Mrs. Yorke's doing. Joseph Poole repaired the furnace in the orangery, and she has managed to coax some of the struggling old flowers within to bloom."

Of course she had. He was beginning to think Mrs. Yorke possessed some manner of magic, and that she had cast a spell on all of Blackwell Abbey. His domestics were filled with cheer. They were efficient, prompt, and happy. There was not a speck of dust to be found anywhere, nor a mouse either. The floors were scrubbed and gleaming. Everything that had been broken was being fixed. His meals were the finest they had ever been. And each time he spied the latest improvement upon his home, a servant was always at hand to merrily inform him that Mrs. Yorke had been responsible for it.

Even Quint had changed during her time at Blackwell Abbey. His moods were no longer quite so black. He curiously found himself lingering in the rooms she had seen decorated, admiring her eye for aesthetics. He wasn't even upset about the impending arrival of his mother, who had sent a telegraph warning him she would soon venture to the northern wilderness he chose to call home in honor of the Christmas season.

"Please tell Mrs. Yorke that she did well in selecting them," he said to Dunreave, shaking himself from his thoughts before thinking better. "Never mind, Dunreave. I'll tell her myself. Do you know where she is?"

"I believe she is in the gardens, Your Grace, fretting with the wreaths."

"In the gardens? With such a chill in the air?" He frowned, not liking the idea of her toiling in the wintry outdoors. "What can she be thinking?"

"I believe she wished to finish them before Her Grace arrives," Dunreave offered.

Quint was already striding to the door that led to the sadly overgrown Blackwell Abbey gardens. Strange that he hadn't bothered to notice how derelict they were until Mrs. Yorke had arrived. But then, he had to admit that there were a great many things he hadn't taken notice of until she had come.

He found her adding ribbon to a circular assortment of fir boughs, bent over her task at one of the wrought-iron tables that were likely older than he was. Small bits of snow were falling from the sky, and the ground was sufficiently cold that they landed in a silvery crust on the gravel. She melded well with the landscape, her black housekeeper's weeds in contrast to the white of the snow, the gray sky beyond ornamented by barren tree branches clawing upward in supplication, punctuated here and there by the occasional snarl of overgrown rosebushes. She was talking to herself, a charming habit he had inadvertently discovered she possessed.

Over the last week, Quint had found himself lingering in halls and walking quietly into rooms and around corners, hoping he might eavesdrop on Mrs. Yorke having a spirited conversation with herself. Why, he couldn't say.

Perhaps the spell she had cast upon his entire household extended to him as well these days.

"No, no," she was murmuring to herself now. "That shall never do. The bow is terribly askew."

The bow looked well enough to him, or at least what little he could see of it from his vantage point over her shoulder. He had halted a measure away from her, content to watch for a few, stolen moments. There was another quality he had noticed his housekeeper possessed. She moved with the natural grace of poetry. Something as simple as the way she smoothed her apron with a lone hand or her brilliant smile of sheer delight when something had gone according to plan —small moments, tiny fragments of her daily toils, and yet each one was laden with such innate beauty and meaning that it robbed him of breath.

To look at Mrs. Yorke was to feel as if one were privy to a grand secret. Quint was reasonably certain his entire household was halfway in love with her in some fashion or another. Watching her in action, he had understood all too clearly how a young beauty of five-and-twenty had ascended the ranks of domestics with such haste.

"Oh, drat," she muttered to herself as the ribbon she had just untied slipped from her grasp and landed on the thin, powdery layer at her feet.

She sank to her knees to retrieve it, her serviceable skirts pooling around her like ink on ivory, and that sight at last jolted Quint into motion. Three more purposeful strides, and he reached her, bending down to retrieve the fallen ribbon, their fingers brushing over one another. His covered in leather, hers marked by the years she'd spent in servitude. Although she didn't know it, his were far more ravaged than hers could ever be.

She gasped, eyes going wide, her polite mask falling into place. "Your Grace. What are you doing in the snow? And look at you, wearing nothing more than your tweed coat. You'll catch a lung infection out here if you don't take care."

"I could say the same of you, Mrs. Yorke," he said pointedly. "Here you are with nary a wrap to keep yourself warm, and you so recently arrived from London to our northern clime."

She tilted her head at him, rather in the fashion of an inquisitive bird. "I was in the kitchens earlier with Cook, and I was quite overheated. I scarcely feel the cold."

But as she said the words, a shiver passed over her.

He frowned, not liking to see her discomfort and not knowing when in the bloody hell the condition of his housekeeper had come to mean so much to him. It merely did.

"You are chilled," he said.

And found himself absurdly mesmerized by a snowflake that had landed on the delicate bridge of her nose. By God, she wasn't even wearing a hat. He had been so starved for the sight of her that he had failed to take note.

The realization was as sobering as it was alarming.

"I've almost finished this wreath," she said with the smile he had come to look forward to each day, the one that made her green eyes sparkle and rendered her loveliness sharper and more acute, almost like a painting coming to life.

She tugged the ribbon from his grasp and stood, continuing with her task quite as if he weren't there at all, on bended knee, one of which was now growing thoroughly soaked from the thin blanket of snow on the gravel. He stood, feeling foolish and awkward and somehow as if their roles had reversed in this enchanted, snow-bedecked world.

He coughed lightly into his gloved hand to cover his discomfit. "Nonetheless, you'll take a chill, madam. I insist you take my coat to warm you."

He shrugged out of the thick country tweed before she could protest.

Her eyes were wide on him, flurries gilding her dark, extravagant eyelashes. "I couldn't, Your Grace."

He placed the garment around her small shoulders despite her words to the contrary. "You mustn't refuse. I insist."

His coat was terribly large, her frame fairly swimming in it and making him realize just how tremendous the size difference between them was. "Thank you."

"You're welcome."

He was dashed cold without it, but the sight of her wearing his coat pleased him beyond words. It was intimate, his garment on her. Shockingly so. And it had him wondering what she might look like draped in nothing more than his shirt, her legs bare beneath its hem.

Like a goddess, he thought. That was what she would look like. And then he instantly castigated himself for such sinful fancies. What was he doing, lusting after his housekeeper yet again?

With a sunny smile, she turned back to her wreath, thankfully oblivious to his reaction to her, which he was incapable of controlling. Clenching his jaw against a stinging rush of shame, he watched as her nimble fingers made short work of tying the ribbon into a bow. He never should have been so familiar in her room, inquiring after whether there was a Mr. Yorke. The moment she had revealed there wasn't one, he had experienced a searing sense of possession he had no right to feel.

Gentlemen did not dally with servants.

Dukes did not lust after their housekeepers.

Quint knew better. And even if he didn't, there was the matter of his hideously scarred hide, which he didn't doubt would frighten away any lover. He had grieved twice when he had lost Amelia. For the lives of her and their child, cut so devastatingly short, and for the man he'd once been, his skin untouched by flame, his heart unblemished by loss.

When he had been healing, he hadn't understood the extent of his injuries. A fiery beam had fallen upon his chest, pinning him in place. He had heaved it away using his hands and all the strength he had, but the damage had been done. His chest, stomach, arms, and hands were ruined.

A gust of wind blew over the park, making the flurries dance around them. Quint shivered, glad he had given Mrs. Yorke his coat. She must have been frozen.

"There we are." Taking up her wreath, Mrs. York spun toward him, her dark skirts swirling around her ankles as she held up her handiwork for his inspection. "What do you think of this, Your Grace?"

He spared a moment for the wreath, taking in the clever way she had mixed fir boughs with holly and sprigs of ivy, pinecones tucked into the lush greenery, her neatly tied ribbon the *pièce de résistance*. But then his gaze settled over her lovely face, noting the way her eyes were even more vibrant than the greens on the wreath and how fine tendrils of black hair had slipped from her coiffure to cling to her cheeks.

"Beautiful," he praised softly.

And he wasn't talking about the wreath. He was talking about her.

Her lips parted, and he feared she had understood the hidden meaning in what he'd just said.

"You'll not object to one of the footmen hanging it on the front door, then?" she asked, dispelling the notion. "For Her Grace's arrival, of course."

Belatedly, it occurred to him that the wreath must be heavy, and he ought to play the gentleman even if his wayward thoughts suggested he was far from one. He stepped forward.

"Allow me to carry it for you, madam."

"It isn't terribly heavy," she denied. "I can manage, though I do thank you, Your Grace. It wouldn't be well done of me to expect the master to carry his own wreath about, now, would it? You'll get sap on your fine clothing and gloves."

It was the first time she had referenced his gloves since the clash they'd had. A flush stole over her cheeks when he didn't immediately respond, telling him she was thinking of that conversation too.

He had been dangerously close to taking her in his arms that day, to testing whether her mouth would fit as perfectly against his as he supposed. To kissing her until they were both breathless and nothing mattered but the two of them, not the past, not the present, and certainly not the future.

"I can manage," she repeated firmly.

"You are always doing everything for the household, Mrs. Yorke," he protested, her determination spurring him into action. "Allow me to do something for you."

Her finely arched brows rose. "It would be wrong of me to allow Your Grace to wait upon me. If you insist, I'll fetch Joseph, and he can take the wreath to the great hall for me."

Quint very adamantly did not want Joseph Poole to intrude upon his time with Mrs. Yorke. "Nonsense. I am perfectly capable of carrying my own wreath to my own front door. Fetching a footman won't be necessary."

Having her to himself was rare. He savored each occasion the way some men did an excellent wine.

Without bothering to await her response, he relieved her of the wreath, the holly garland poking him even through the barrier of his leather gloves, landing its barb in a particularly sensitive spot.

"Yow!"

The exclamation fled him before he could stop it, and he nearly lost the wreath but saved it at the last moment.

"What is the matter, Your Grace?"

"The holly," he admitted ruefully. "I do believe it was getting even with me for having been made to sacrifice itself for the embellishment of my door."

"It is deceptively prickly, is it not? Shall I take it from you?"

He stared at her hands. "You were holding the wreath. Did the holly not stab you?"

"Oh no, Your Grace." She smiled, showing him her palms, which were mottled and scarred. "My hands are toughened from my years in service. When I was a maid of all work, I had to do the scullery. More than one incident with boiling water has rendered much of my hands numb. A bit of holly is no match for me."

A sudden, almost violent desire to drop the wreath and take her hands in his assailed him, so strong and vehement he had to swallow hard against a rush of longing. He loathed the thought of her enduring the pain of such scalding burns, the difficult life in service she'd endured already for one so young. But he also admired her for her steadfast perseverance.

He knew without asking that she would have worked with those raw, burned hands. That it was a miracle they hadn't festered, given all the duties she must have had.

"I insist on carrying it," Quint managed, struck by the fervent wish that their circumstances were different.

That he wasn't a duke and she was not his housekeeper. That he wasn't hideously scarred and embittered, that she was not working herself to the bone in service. That they were man and woman, unencumbered, and he would be free to speak with her, to court her.

But that was yet another foolish notion, and he ought to have known better.

Turning away from her, he strode back toward the manor house, his footfalls crunching on the gravel and snow, wind whipping cold air against his cheeks as he bore the wreath like an albatross. A footman was waiting, opening the door. Quint held back, allowing for Mrs. Yorke to precede him. Had the entire household seen him chase after her out to the gardens? He needed to take greater care, it would seem, for the last thing he wanted to do was cause gossip belowstairs by exhibiting favoritism where she was concerned.

He trailed after her through the maze of corridors to the great hall and then out the front door, where he could finally relieve himself of his burden by hanging the wreath on a brass hook mounted to the panel for just such a purpose. The wind whipped up just as Mrs. Yorke stepped past him, straightening the bow to her liking. They stood in such proximity that a silken tendril of her hair brushed over his cheek.

The startling intimacy sent desire crashing over him.

She cast a bright smile at him. "There. It is perfect, is it not?"

"Perfect," he agreed tightly.

But once again, it wasn't the blasted wreath he was speaking of.

∼

"Mrs. Yorke?"

At Mary's voice, Joceline jumped, startled from her reverie. She had been overseeing the airing out of the bedchamber the dowager duchess would be using, a room that had been sealed up for what was obviously a considerable amount of time. It wasn't the task that had given her pause, sending her mind wandering, however. Rather, it had been the realization that the room had quite plainly belonged to another woman. A woman whose belongings had been sealed away, and yet whose watercolors and pictures and other belongings had been left quite as if their original owner had left the room for a moment, intending to return.

"Yes, Mary?" Joceline asked, unable to dispel the heaviness in her heart.

This room had belonged to the duke's wife.

"What am I to do with the jewelry case?" Mary asked as, around them, maids removed coverings from furniture and dusted and mopped.

"I'll need to speak with His Grace," she said, wondering how she was to handle such a delicate matter.

She had never needed to inquire about the belongings of a dead spouse at any of her previous situations. Navigating such a treacherous subject would be difficult enough with anyone, let alone the Duke of Sedgewick.

"Leave it where it is for now," she added. "The duchess's belongings are to remain where they are until I tell you otherwise."

"Of course, Mrs. Yorke," Mary said agreeably.

Joceline sighed. The dowager was to arrive soon, and they couldn't afford to lose any time in their preparations. She was going to have to seek out the duke now so that the maids she had delegated to the room opening could complete their duties.

"See that the maids carry on while I'm gone," she instructed Mary.

The walk through the servants' stair and halls felt as if it took an eternity, dread weighing heavily upon her. Over her short tenure at Blackwell Abbey, she had made astonishing leaps where the duke was concerned. She feared undoing all the progress with the uncomfortable interview that was bound to ensue.

Finding Sedgewick was yet another adventure as she emerged to the great hall. He was not in his study where she had expected him to be at this hour. Nor was he out riding, she discovered after inquiring with Dunreave. The duke was, astonishingly enough, in his library.

Joceline sought him there, knocking lightly at the door before he bade her to enter. She crossed the threshold, offering him a curtsy.

"Your Grace."

"Mrs. Yorke," he greeted, his voice lacking the ice she had come to expect.

In fact, unless she was mistaken, there was just the tiniest hint of warmth in his baritone. She clutched her skirts tightly, nervousness creeping over her. A cold, frosty Duke of Sedgewick felt somehow easier to face, given the very personal nature of the news she was about to impart.

Standing by the wall of books, he was dressed informally in shirtsleeves and a waistcoat paired with tweed trousers that hugged his long, lean legs, his dark-gold hair brushing his shoulders. The leather gloves that were perpetually in place obscured her view of his large hands as he plucked the spine of a book from its shelf and opened it to examine the frontispiece, quite as if they had all the time in the world for a leisurely conversation.

The action reminded her that she was standing at the threshold staring at him like a dolt. She hadn't come to the library to swoon over the duke's undeniably handsome form. Nor had she come to ogle him as if she were some innocent debutante meeting her first suitor. The Duke of Sedgewick was her employer, and she was his housekeeper. Their worlds were as disparate as summer and winter. She must not forget it.

"If Your Grace has the time to speak with me, I require some direction concerning the bedchamber we are preparing for Her Grace," she said, gratified that her voice sounded calm and smooth when, inwardly, she felt anything but.

He lowered the book, his unusual gaze intent upon hers. "Whatever the matter is, I trust your judgment, Mrs. Yorke. You have my leave to do whatever you must."

His mild trust in her only served to heighten her worry.

She clenched her skirts even more tightly, her knuckles aching. "Forgive me, Your Grace. It wasn't my intention to trouble you this morning. However, I chose the largest of the closed bedrooms for Her Grace's comfort, and it would appear that the chamber belonged to…another."

His expression instantly changed, his bearing stiffening as he snapped the book closed. "The household has distinct orders that the duchess's bedchamber is not to be disturbed."

"Perhaps the household once did, but in the absence of a former housekeeper to consult, the order was never conveyed to me," she countered gently. "I was simply seeing to the opening of the room that seemed best suited to Her Grace."

He tossed the book to a nearby table without regard for its binding. "You have opened it?" he demanded sharply.

Oh dear. Here he was, the Duke of Sedgewick returned. A snarling beast who would as soon bite as accept a hint of kindness.

"I-I am sorry, Your Grace," she stammered. "I will see to it that the maids close it at once. Is there another room that is appropriate for Her Grace? We will ready the chamber of your choice instead."

But he was already stalking past her, his countenance hewn in granite.

"Your Grace?"

"Attend to your other duties, Mrs. Yorke," he bit out over his shoulder, his booted strides taking him to the threshold. "I'll see to the room myself."

Instinctively, Joceline hastened after him, not wanting him to bellow and frighten her maids when she was at fault for this dreadful mistake. She couldn't chase after him, however, so she flitted back into the servants' stair and took the steps two at a time, her skirts hiked in an undignified display she had no time to worry over. She was breathless by the time she reached the duchess's bedroom, the duke stalking down the opposite end of the hall like a thunderstorm about to unleash a torrent.

"Stop," she cried breathlessly when she reached the threshold.

All eyes turned to her, the chatter and flurry of movements abruptly ceasing.

"Out, all of you," she directed. "At once."

"But, Mrs. Yorke," Mary protested, "we were just beginning to—"

"Resume your routine duties for the day," she interrupted sharply, aware that they had a scant few moments before the duke arrived. "Be gone."

"Yes, Mrs. Yorke."

The maids filed from the bedchamber past her, moving toward the servants' stair she had recently exited. And none too soon. The last maid had just disappeared behind the safety of the closed door when Sedgewick reached her.

"Chasing away your precious little chicks before the evil wolf arrives?" he asked snidely.

THE DUKE WHO DESPISED CHRISTMAS

She had clearly violated their temporary pax. The man who had carried the holly wreath for her despite the thorny pricks of its glossy leaves was nowhere to be seen now. In his place was the same man who had sacked her for decorating his drawing room with greenery and Christmas trees.

"I was merely trying to ameliorate the damage I've inadvertently done," she defended.

"Such a pretty vocabulary you have, Mrs. Yorke," he mocked.

She would not be intimidated by him, however. "Thank you, Your Grace. I'm honored you noticed."

His eyes narrowed. "Why did you dismiss the maids?"

"Because I didn't want them to suffer for my mistake," she answered honestly. "I am to blame for what happened, not them. I alone will bear the burden. Please know, Your Grace, that it was never my intention to cause you so much upset."

"Upset," he spat. "That is a tepid word for what I'm feeling right now, madam."

Beneath his fury and ice, Joceline sensed the depth of his sadness. It was there in the shadows of his blue-green eyes. He wasn't a wolf or a beast at all in that moment. He was a man devastated by grief, haunted by the wraiths of his past, determined to seal his emotions away the same as he had his dead wife's room.

"I'll restore the chamber, Your Grace," she reassured him quietly. "You may return to the library."

His lip curled. "Do you truly have the temerity to order me about in my own home, Mrs. Yorke?"

Had she been ordering him? No, she rather thought she had been encouraging him. But he was in a desperately dark mood, and there would be no appeasing him in this condition.

"Of course not, Your Grace. I beg your pardon. I merely wished for you to know that there isn't a need for you to worry a moment more about this unfortunate incident. I'll rectify matters on my own."

With a curtsy, she attempted to move past him, intending to apply furniture coverings and put everything back in its proper place. But he blocked her with his big, impassive frame.

"I'll do it," he said.

"Your Grace should not be tasked with such a duty," she countered. "I am at fault. Allow me to—"

"I said, I will do it," he interrupted, his voice harsh and cold. "Leave me, Mrs. Yorke."

She had no choice but to obey him. The stony, bleak expression on his face told her that she didn't dare to defy him in this.

Joceline nodded. "Of course, Your Grace."

She dipped into a curtsy before gathering up her skirts and fleeing just as the maids had done some minutes before.

Leaving him to the memories he had sealed inside his dead wife's room and the pain of the past. And though she knew she had no right to feel it, Joceline couldn't shake the sensation that she was abandoning him as she descended the servants' stair. Her foolish heart gave a pang, but she tamped it down, along with old hopes she'd believed long gone.

CHAPTER 6

Quint didn't know how long he'd been sitting in Amelia's bedchamber, surrounded by the disarray of her personal effects, which had been moved about by well-intentioned maids in their efforts to dust, uncover, and organize. She had used the room whenever they'd been in residence, which hadn't been often. Amelia had far preferred London or Sedgewick Manor in Buckinghamshire to Blackwell Abbey, which was admittedly a crumbling relic from centuries past. The northern clime had been a source of displeasure for her, along with the cumbersome train journey.

It had been her dislike of the estate that had led him here, after the fire at Sedgewick Manor, which had ravaged the eastern wing and taken Amelia's and their baby's life in the process. A place of fewer memories. Four walls that would not smell like smoke or be a daily reminder of all he had lost that day. He had forgotten, in fact, how many of her belongings had remained when he had given the order to his then-housekeeper to seal the room and its contents away.

For two years, it had remained untouched. Undisturbed. And now, it had been reopened, its curtains tied back to allow sunlight to stream into the mullioned windows, the coverings removed from the furniture and wall hangings. Amelia's picture stared back at him from a small gilt frame atop a table. Her watercolors, all ethereal landscapes she had painted during her time at Blackwell Abbey, dotted the walls. A case of her jewelry was laid out as if she were preparing her toilette, a bottle of her scent nearby. He had no doubt that if he inspected the wardrobe, he would find more bits and pieces of her remaining—warm winter gowns, underpinnings, God knew what else, and Quint didn't have the heart to look.

He had been an idiot to think this day would never come. He realized that now as he stripped the leather gloves from his hands and laid them aside. The door was closed, and he had no fear of his hideous scars being viewed. No one had dared return, not even the intrepid Mrs. Yorke, who had invaded his home just as she had this room, upsetting his peace.

Ah, Mrs. Yorke.

She infuriated him. She irritated him. She intrigued him.

The woman was a problem. Earlier, when she had come to him in his library, he had been seized by the wild, incredibly stupid notion that he should invite her to sit with him. That they might discuss books or poetry or anything of interest. He hadn't known just how hungry he was for female companionship, how very starved for it, until her arrival. He knew it now, thanks to her. Knew it as he sat in the midst of his dead wife's room, surveying all that remained of her.

And he hated himself for that weakness, for the betrayal of Amelia's memory. He hadn't been able to save her from the fire that awful day. The least he could do was remain constant to her in death, yet he had been caught in the thrall of his housekeeper, of all people. He had been thinking about kissing, touching, and Lord help him, so much more than that.

Quint closed his eyes and heaved a heavy sigh, scrubbing a hand along his jaw. "Forgive me, Amelia. Forgive me for failing you in every way."

He opened his eyes, and no one was there but the watercolors and the picture, Amelia dressed in a beautiful Worth gown, flowers in her hair, eyes sparkling with the vivacity he had forgotten how much he missed. Once, there had been lightness in his life. There had been laughter and picnics and discussions of Shakespeare. There had been walks through the countryside and rides on Rotten Row and dancing with her in his arms beneath glittering chandeliers. There had been the hope of a family, about to begin before her life had been taken far too soon, the new life in her womb going with her.

Now, there was an empty room filled with objects. There was the grief that threatened to consume him. The guilt that he had failed her and their child both. There were two long years, a yawning fissure between his old life and the man he was now.

There was the closed door clicking open and Mrs. Yorke standing at the threshold, her eyes wide with shock.

"Your Grace," she said. "Forgive me. I thought you were no longer within the chamber. I will leave you to your peace."

Quint didn't know what prompted him to shoot to his feet, but he was suddenly standing. "Wait."

She hesitated, lingering, eyes fringed with lush, dark lashes, heart-shaped face impossibly pretty. "Yes, Your Grace?"

"There is no peace in this room," he told her. "You may as

well come in, and I'll give you some direction on what is to be done with the contents of the chamber."

"Of course." She crossed the threshold, the door naturally gliding closed at her back.

When she entered the room, it was as if the heavy weight upon his chest lifted and he could breathe again. He despised the effect this woman had upon him. He hated himself for acknowledging it.

And yet, it simply was.

"The pictures should all be taken down," he said, struggling to keep his voice from cracking beneath the tremendous, twin weights of regret and grief. "See that they are stored in the attics where they will be well protected and covered."

"I will see that they are packed away with great care, Your Grace."

Her voice was calm, soothing. Pleasant. Edged with sympathy he didn't deserve.

"Thank you, madam. The furniture may remain for my mother's use. Bring in pictures for the walls from other bedrooms if you must. The rest of my wife's belongings may be packed away as well."

Difficult words to say. Necessary words. He could not live in the past. For so long, he had been unable to force himself to address these lingering parts of Amelia. To admit to himself that she would never return. To celebrate Christmas without her. To live again.

Perhaps the time had come to do both.

"I'll see to that as well, Your Grace," Mrs. Yorke said, her calm efficiency helping to soothe his jagged nerves.

"Thank you." Belatedly, he recalled that he wasn't wearing his gloves. They remained on the table behind him. He flexed his scarred fingers, feeling the familiar tightness of the fire-damaged skin.

Her vibrant, green gaze dipped to his hands, and his gut clenched as he awaited her reaction, her revulsion. But she exhibited neither disgust nor shock, her expression never changing as her eyes returned to his.

"You needn't thank me, Your Grace. I'm sorry for my mishandling of the circumstances this morning. Am I to understand that you wish for the dowager to be given this room after all?"

"Yes," he told her, his voice tight with suppressed emotions, the single-word response all he could manage.

"I will direct the maids to return, then, supposing Your Grace finds it acceptable to do so?"

"Of course, Mrs. Yorke. Do whatever you must. I only ask that you are discreet with the removal. I haven't been in this room in over two years, and I'm feeling somewhat…overwrought."

"I understand," she told him softly.

And he knew that she did, in her own way. She had lost her father. Had been thrust from the bosom of her loving home and into service, denied the life she might have had, the husband and family that may have one day been hers. He swallowed hard against a fresh wave of unwanted emotion, snatched up his gloves, and left the room without another word before he did or said something truly reckless.

∽

JOCELINE EMERGED FROM THE SERVANTS' stair that evening after dinner, feet sore, back aching, heart heavy. She had personally overseen the packing of the former duchess's pictures, making certain that each one was well wrapped in cloths before assigning them to footmen who waited to carry them into the attics for safekeeping. With each watercolor, she had felt another piece of her heart breaking for the Duke of Sedgewick, understanding how painful it must have been for him to be surrounded by the remnants of his wife's things after he had avoided them for so long.

But it wasn't just the duke's heartbreak that had affected her through the long hours of somber removal. It was the secret they shared as well. When she had ventured back to the duchess's bedchamber, he hadn't been wearing his gloves. Nor had he bothered to put them back on. Instead, he had stood before her, his scars there for her to see, his grief unfettered. He had been a broken man, one who had loved his wife very much. One who had been vulnerable instead of formidable, weary instead of icy. And he had allowed her to see a part of him he kept from others, as if he had shared a secret that was theirs alone.

Fanciful thinking on her part, she knew, but the bond she couldn't help but to feel between herself and the Duke of Sedgewick seemed to grow exponentially with each passing day. Or perhaps it was merely *her* feeling that bond, imagining it existed. Either way, she would never know. Housekeepers and dukes didn't cross boundaries. She was here to manage his household, not to develop tender feelings for the man. Besides, he had clearly been hopelessly in love with his wife. It was wrong of her, but she couldn't quite quell a sudden stab of envy, not without its accompanying guilt. Who was she, who had no place in the Duke of Sedgewick's life, to be jealous of his dead wife?

As she passed His Grace's study, the low rumble of his voice took her by surprise.

"Mrs. Yorke," he called.

She halted, turning to find his door partially ajar, the duke seated at his desk in the slant of the opened door. "Do you need me for something, Your Grace?"

"Come inside, if you please," he invited with an odd half smile on his beautifully sculpted lips.

She did as he asked, hesitating near the open door, all too aware of how dangerously handsome he was and how inappropriate her feelings were where he was concerned. She felt something for him. A tenderness she'd never felt for another. A deep pull of attraction.

"How may I be of service?" she asked brightly, banishing those wicked thoughts.

"Close the door, if you please."

Joceline did as he asked, wondering at the reason even as an illicit surge of anticipation went through her at the prospect of being alone with him. But there was also an edge of concern. Would he decide to give her the sack for her overstepping after all?

She turned to face him, dipping a curtsy, belatedly remembering herself. "Your Grace."

"You needn't linger at the door as if I'm a lion about to pounce," he said, waving a gloved hand to indicate she should take one of the chairs opposite his desk. "Come and have a seat, if you please."

He was being polite, she noted warily, but his gloves were firmly back in place. She wished that they were gone, for they seemed like yet another barrier he had erected to keep the world at a safe distance. And although she had no right to want to tear down those walls, she still did.

Joceline seated herself primly and folded her hands in her lap. "What does Your Grace require?"

"Some company," he said wryly. "Just for a few moments."

That was when she noticed a half-empty glass of brandy on his desk. He had been imbibing, which was most unlike him.

"Of course," she said simply, trying not to frown at the evidence that he had been so deeply affected by the bedchamber's reopening.

Her fault.

"Would you like a brandy, Mrs. Yorke?" he inquired, obviously having caught her eyeing the liquor.

"It would be most improper, Your Grace."

"That isn't what I asked you." His mien was calm, assessing, his gaze as intense as ever.

"I fear such an elixir would be far too strong," she hedged.

"A brandy and soda water, then," he suggested. "Spare me the misery of drinking alone."

"Surely there is a more suitable companion for the task," she suggested kindly, fearing what would happen if she lingered, partook in spirits with him, and allowed her own defenses to fall. "Dunreave, perhaps?"

"A teetotaler, if you would believe it." The duke raised an imperious brow. "So, you see, it is either you or one of the footmen, and without paying insult to Joseph or Peter, I would far prefer you as my accompaniment to either of them."

"Very well, then," she relented with the greatest of reluctance. "A brandy and soda water, and if Mr. Dunreave takes me to task, I shall endure his disapproval."

"He won't take you to task," the duke was quick to insist, rising and going to a sideboard where glasses and bottles were housed. In her time here, the levels of the liquids contained within had failed to move.

With a deft hand, he prepared her drink whilst Joceline sat uncomfortably in her chair, aware of how awkward and unusual her present circumstances were. Never in all her years of service had the gentleman of the house ever invited her to sit with him in his study. And certainly not to imbibe together.

But the Duke of Sedgewick had asked, and the Duke of Sedgewick would get what he wanted.

He returned to her, offering the glass. She accepted it, her fingers brushing over soft leather, wishing it were his bare skin instead. She wondered why he insisted upon hiding his hands. Was it because he was embarrassed by his scars, or was it too painful for him to see them, a reminder of how he had received them?

"Here you are."

"Thank you, Your Grace."

Sedgewick settled in his seat, lifting his drink to her in toast. "No, my dear Mrs. Yorke. I am the grateful one. I ought to be thanking you, rather than the other way around."

She had raised her glass in turn, but now she clenched the stem in a tight grip, frozen by the frank admiration in his eyes. He was looking at her in a way a man should never look at his housekeeper. And she liked it. Liked it far too much.

"I am here at Blackwell Abbey to perform a duty," she reminded him. "Nothing more."

"And at my mother's behest, no less." He raised his glass to his lips, taking a healthy swallow. "Ah, the irony."

She wasn't sure what she ought to say to such a statement, so she took up her brandy and soda water, sipping delicately at it. She'd had spirits before, but not often. There was no place in her life for excess. Still, the drink was surprisingly pleasant.

"I expect you must think me a monster," he said. "My temper hasn't always been this mercurial, I assure you. Only since the fire."

"It wouldn't be my place to think poorly of you, Your Grace," she said with loyal resolve. "A housekeeper's lot is to serve, never to judge."

"Yes, but you are a woman as well, aren't you, Mrs. Yorke?" His gaze was shrewd and knowing.

For a moment, she feared she had allowed too much of her feelings to show in her expression. She had always been so carefully guarded. It came with the territory of being in service. One could never afford to allow one's true opinions or feelings to be known. One merely served.

"I am a housekeeper first," she asserted, gripping her glass tightly again.

"Perhaps we can call a truce for a small time," he suggested. "Here in this study, you may place the housekeeper aside. No Mrs. Yorke for a few minutes. Instead, you will merely be..."

His words trailed away, and he watched her with silent expectation.

It occurred to her that he wanted her given name, which was thoroughly improper. Becoming too familiar with one's employer was a grave mistake.

"I'm sure I shouldn't say, Your Grace."

"Shouldn't or won't?" he asked, his voice silken. "Come now. Earlier, I allowed you to see a part of me that few others have seen. In return, I think it only fair that you tell me your given name."

He had her there, and the expression on his face—calmly patient—told her he knew it.

"Joceline," she allowed. "My name is Joceline, Your Grace."

He repeated her name slowly, as if testing its feeling on his tongue, and she had never thought it a lovely or particularly interesting name, but when the Duke of Sedgewick said it in his deep, velvety baritone, she thought it sounded like the loveliest name in the world.

"The name suits you, I think." He nodded, lifting his glass again. "A toast to you, Joceline. In a scant few weeks, you have managed to do what none of your predecessors have done."

Heat blossomed on her cheeks. "Perhaps it was not the right time, Your Grace."

"Or perhaps it was not the right woman for the job," he suggested. "Hear, hear."

She raised her glass because he wanted her to, a complex web of emotion tangling around her. His praise was heady. So, too, the way he was looking at her. His use of her given name. The privacy of the study, the door closed behind them. The intimacy of a shared drink and secrets.

They had ventured into territory most treacherous, and she knew it.

Joceline took a longer drink from her brandy and soda water, sparing herself the need to answer him. He drank his brandy as well, his gaze never straying from her. It was most disconcerting. Impossibly intimate, and yet they were not even touching, simply sitting on opposite sides of his desk in a room that smelled like the pleasing warmth of the fireplace and his musky ambergris scent.

"I suppose you must be wondering about my scars," he said suddenly, breaking the companionable silence that had fallen between them.

"I would never presume to do so, Your Grace," she hastened to say.

"A politic response." He gave her a thin smile that didn't reach his eyes. "But curiosity is natural. You've already commented on my gloves. Now you've seen the reason."

"I'm afraid I still don't understand," Joceline blurted, the brandy and soda water loosening her tongue.

She wasn't accustomed to spirits. What had she been thinking? Best not to drink another drop.

"You don't?"

She shook her head, holding his regard, in for a penny, in for a pound. "No."

Setting his glass down on the polished surface of his desk, he then reached for his left glove, plucking it away to reveal the scarred hand beneath. The right glove came next, leaving both hands revealed to her. At this proximity, she could see the extent of the damage that had been done by flame.

"Do you know how she died, Joceline?" he asked, his use of her name sending a jolt through her.

She swallowed, realizing he was speaking of his wife. "Of course not, and you needn't speak of such a distressing subject."

"I want to, however." He lightly stroked the desk with his damaged fingertips, as if he were touching it for the first time, such reverence. "This morning taught me that perhaps I need to, that I've been hiding from the past for far too long and it's time I faced it."

"If unburdening yourself to me would be of assistance to you, I'd be honored to listen," she said, meaning those words far more than she should.

What she felt for the Duke of Sedgewick went beyond the caring a housekeeper would have for her employer. She had seen past the curt, icy mask to the real man suffering beneath. His grief and anger had led him to become a recluse, but there was so much more to him than that.

"My wife died in a fire at Sedgewick Hall three weeks before Christmas Day," he said, the raw pain in his voice wrapping itself around her heart like a vise. "I had gone out for a ride that morning. I returned home to smoke billowing from the eastern wing. I rushed inside and was told by the servants that she had gone to that wing in search of the old nursery. She was expecting, you see. She'd taken an oil lamp with her because that part of the house wasn't plumbed for gaslights. Somehow, it must have upended."

"My God," she said, pressing a hand over her mouth as horror unfurled. So much made sense, all the pieces of him coming together.

"I tried to reach her," he continued, his gaze taking on a faraway look. "The footmen were gathering water buckets from the pond, but it wasn't enough. By the time I raced to the east wing, the whole structure had begun to fail. The floor collapsed, and a burning beam fell across my chest, pinning me. It required all the strength I had to push it away. I was still intent upon finding her, but some of the footmen came and dragged me from the rubble. It was too late to save her. I hide my scars not just because they are hideous, but because they're a reminder of my failure. They died that day because of me."

Sweet heavens, the poor man. Little wonder he had been tormented. He believed he was responsible for the deaths of his wife and unborn child. Before Joceline could think twice over the familiarity of her gesture, she leaned forward in her chair and laid her hands over his on the desk. Beneath her work-roughened fingertips, the evidence of his valiant fight to save the woman he loved was smooth yet rippled.

"You tried to save them and were nearly killed," she said softly. "You did everything you could."

"I should have been there," he insisted stubbornly. "If I hadn't been riding…"

"If you hadn't been riding, would it have happened any differently?" she asked, keeping her voice gentle.

For such a large, impassive, arrogant man, he seemed so very vulnerable in this moment of dark confession, as if he needed all the strength she could give him.

"I don't know," he admitted hoarsely. "The questions, what might have been, the guilt of being pulled from the flames alive when she and the baby she carried were left to burn…they haunt me as much as the scars do."

"You've been punishing yourself, but you don't deserve to do penance. I am certain that your wife must have loved you, and that she wouldn't have wished for you to suffer in her absence."

He stared at her, saying nothing, and for a wild moment,

Joceline feared she had gone too far. That the price for her sympathy would be her situation, and she would finally find herself on the next train to London before the dowager arrived. That all her work here would have been for naught, and she would have scarcely anything to send home to Mama and her siblings.

But then he spoke at last, his voice as raw as she'd ever heard it. "You are too kind to me. I don't deserve it."

"Yes," she countered, her heart breaking anew for him, "you do."

"I've been a beast to you, and meanwhile, you have been nothing short of an angel, heaven-sent." He moved suddenly, taking her hands in his and bowing over them, pressing a fervent kiss to the top of first one, then another.

"I-I haven't," she protested, breathless. "I can assure you I'm no angel."

Sparks seemed to shoot past her wrists, skipping up her elbow, making her giddy. The touch of his mouth on her bare skin felt hot and forbidden. The sight of his proud lips on her work-chapped hand, the connection of his gaze searing into hers like a touch of its own, pulled her nearer, into his web. The air between them had shifted from grief to heated awareness.

"Joceline," he murmured, turning one hand over and kissing the center of her palm, then higher still, to her wrist.

His mouth was a brand, burning, tempting. She wanted to revel in these stolen moments, in his touch, his lips. Wanted to throw herself across his desk and into his arms. But then she saw the slumberous cast of his eyes, his pupils dilated, and she understood that he was in his cups. That he had sought to drown his sorrows in brandy, and to allow a moment more of anything illicit to continue between them would be wrong.

She pulled her hands from his grasp and stood with haste,

fleeing from the study without a thought for formality or the damage she might be doing to herself in running away. She didn't stop until she had reached her small, cold housekeeper's room.

And it was only then that she allowed herself to weep, shedding tears for the Duke of Sedgewick, for his lost wife and child, and for what could never be.

CHAPTER 7

Quint had made a grievous mistake.

He had known it the night before when he had been so caught up in the moment and in Mrs. Yorke —*Joceline*—that he had allowed himself to not just touch her hands, but kiss them. He had known it as he'd watched her flee his study in a swirl of dark, serviceable skirts and crisp white apron, her chatelaine jingling as if in reproach with each step. He'd known it later as he had lain awake in his bed, his lips still tingling with the memory of his mouth on her bare skin. He'd known it as his cock had hardened to thoughts of what he might do with her, were they anyone other than who they were.

And he knew it now as he awaited her in his library, surrounded by the merry Yuletide decorations she had festooned about.

Unable to remain still, he paced the Axminster, scrubbing at his jaw with a gloved hand, so many confusing, complex emotions roiling within him. There was guilt over desiring another woman, and one who was forbidden to him at that. There was shame over having made overtures when he did

THE DUKE WHO DESPISED CHRISTMAS

not know if they were welcomed. There was the anguish of his past colliding with the undeniable force of his future.

God, there was so much. So bloody much. And it threatened to consume him. He wanted Joceline. He could not have her. Everything that had been hateful to him was now somehow comforting and desirable—a woman's touch, his skin on hers, the revelation of his scars, the Christmas greenery, a Yuletide season unmarred by loss and pain. Hell, he didn't even mind that his mother was set to arrive soon. When last he had seen her, they'd had a row over his insistence upon hiding away in the north. She had wanted him to return to London and resume his duties. The notion had made him want to retch. That had been a year ago when she had ventured to Blackwell Abbey, only to return to polite society disappointed.

And now…

Well, now, the prospect of resuming his own life—albeit a very changed one—no longer seemed so intolerable. If anything, it felt *hopeful*. He had Joceline Yorke to thank for that, a capable, beautiful, resilient woman who had upended his sheltered world when she had come to Blackwell Abbey. A woman he owed an apology to for his behavior the previous evening.

A knock sounded at the closed door, a sharp, distinct rap he had come to recognize as hers.

"Enter," he called, turning on his heel so that he would be facing her.

A click, the slow sweep of the portal, and then she was there on the threshold, unfairly gorgeous with her inky tresses pulled into a neat chignon, today's dove-gray gown far too staid a color. She deserved to wear rich, bold silks instead of plain wool, jewel-toned hues like emerald to match her eyes and ruby and sapphire. What a travesty it was that she had never been given a Season or a chance to make a proper match, but had instead been sent to service, waiting upon the whims of others.

"Your Grace," she said solemnly, dipping into a curtsy, her formality firmly in place.

Quite as if he had never asked her to sit with him in his study and partake in brandy—an act itself that was unconscionable for the master of the house. He could blame the rawness of his emotions and the effect of the spirits he so rarely imbibed, but the truth was, it was also her.

"Mrs. Yorke," he greeted in turn. "Please, come in."

"The door, Your Grace?" she asked, her eyes questioning.

Good God, he hoped she was not uncomfortable being alone with him after yesterday. "Close it, if you please."

She did so, venturing into the room in an elegant glide but stopping at a safe distance. "What does Your Grace require this afternoon?"

"You have my assurance that nothing untoward will occur, Mrs. Yorke," he told her. "Not this afternoon, nor ever again. Pray accept my most sincere apologies for what happened last night. I overstepped my bounds, and I must humbly ask for your forgiveness."

An expression of surprise flitted over her countenance. "You need not apologize. You are lonely, and your grief and the brandy were clouding your judgment. I understand."

"I *am* lonely," he agreed roughly, the confession torn from him. "But it wasn't the grief and the brandy that moved me. It was you. However, regardless of what I feel, you have my promise that I'll not make any further overtures. Your position is secure. I'll not force myself upon you again."

Something shifted in her expression. "Is that what you think, Your Grace? That you forced yourself upon me?"

Seething self-loathing rose like a tide. "Of course. I should never have asked you to join me for brandy. Nor should I have deigned to touch you. My actions were improper and inexcusable. I understand why you ran from my study. I vow it won't happen again."

She shook her head slowly, moving nearer to him, so that she was close enough to touch and her clean scent of floral soap tantalized him. "That isn't why I fled your study last evening."

A sharp pang of uncontrollable longing almost robbed him of breath.

"It isn't?" he rasped.

"No." Her green eyes sparkled in the late-day sunlight filtering through the windows, and he found himself mesmerized by the hints of copper and gold flecking her irises, by the shadowy sweep of her long lashes. "I left because you were in your cups, and I didn't want to take advantage of your grief or your vulnerability."

His vulnerability.

Not long ago, he would have laughed bitterly at such a notion. For he had believed himself hardened. Impervious. He had believed himself as wizened as one of the ancient oaks ringing the Blackwell Abbey park. But Joceline had changed that. She'd somehow dismantled all his walls, tearing them down until he realized he did still have a heart beating in his chest. That he hadn't died that awful day two years ago.

And that perhaps there might be a chance he could feel again.

"I wasn't so soused that I didn't know what I was doing," he confessed. "If anyone was taking advantage, it was me. You're my housekeeper. I'm your employer. You're young and innocent. I'm…neither of those things. It was unfair of me to press my suit."

He felt every bit of his five-and-thirty years in this moment. More than that. He felt ancient compared to her. He was a decade her senior. Why hadn't their age disparity occurred to him until now? Likely, he'd been too preoccupied with their social positions, with his own soul-shattering guilt and grief.

Selfish. That was what he was. He was still alive, when Amelia and their baby were forever lost to him. And here he stood, lusting after a young housekeeper.

He hated himself.

"What if I told you that your attention was welcome?" she asked softly.

A rush of yearning crashed into Quint, so fierce that his knees almost trembled from the force of it. "Mrs. Yorke. Joceline. What are you saying?"

"I'm saying that I wanted what happened," she said, laying a hand on his jaw, her touch warm and tender. "I wanted more than that to happen, Your Grace. I know it's wrong of me. I have no right to feel the way I do for you, and yet I can't seem to help it."

"Quint," he told her roughly. "Call me Quint."

For somehow, it seemed wrong of her to continue with his title, to uphold the premise of civility, when they had both ventured well beyond the bounds of formality. Everything changed with these mutual confessions. They could never go back to who they had been before. They were Quint and Joceline now, here in this stolen moment, in the haven of his library, where it was no one but the two of them.

"Quint," she repeated, and then she did something utterly astonishing.

She rose on her toes, sealing her mouth to his, her hand still on his jaw.

His reaction was instant and instinctive. He cupped her face as he pressed his lips over hers. And sweet God, *her lips*. They were as lush and sweet and soft as he had imagined. They moved against his, beneath his, a revelation for which he found himself wholly unprepared. For a moment, he simply kissed her, his mouth taking what he needed from hers, all the succor, the comfort, the silken heat. But then he couldn't resist teasing her lips open, his tongue sliding deep to taste her, to draw as much of her inside himself as he could.

She made a low, throaty sound, and then somehow, they were moving. Moving together, as if they were of one mind. Never taking his lips from hers, he guided Joceline backward to a nearby table, where some bric-a-brac was his only impediment to lifting her atop it. He swept it to the floor with an impatient swipe of his arm, dimly cognizant of the sound of breaking glass. Whatever it was, he didn't care. It didn't matter more than kissing her. Nothing could.

He grasped her waist and lifted her with ease, settling her on the table so that she was even with his height, all the better for him to ravish her mouth. Because he was suddenly ravenous for her. All the restraint he had been clinging to where she was concerned had been obliterated the instant she had kissed him.

She tasted sweet, like the afternoon tea she must have consumed, her tongue shyly moving against his. He was reminded that she was younger, certainly less experienced than he, and tore his mouth from hers, staring down at her with ragged breath.

"Forgive me," he managed. "I lost my head when your lips touched mine. I shouldn't be so rough with you."

"There's nothing to forgive," she told him. "And you're anything but rough. I like the way you kiss me."

"Good," he gritted, taking her mouth again.

This time, he tried to kiss her more gently, to smooth his lips over hers in slow, determined seduction rather than devouring her. But it was difficult. He wanted Joceline with a ferocity that terrified him. He wanted her despite all the reasons he shouldn't.

Wanted her desperately.

She draped her arms about his neck, one of her legs wrapping around his hip to draw him closer. And he accepted her invitation, pulling her to the edge of the table so that he could align his rigid length with the apex of her thighs. Although the barrier of skirts and petticoats and apron remained, he moaned into her kiss, giving her his tongue once more.

He was a beast again, but a different sort than the one he'd been. This beast was consumed by desire, his heart pounding, blood heated, the ache of need so sharp in his ballocks that he sucked in a breath as his cock ground against her voluminous skirts, seeking more of her. Seeking her sex.

The thought of flipping up her skirts and teasing the soft petals of her sex had him straining against her. He couldn't do that, of course. This was too much, too quickly, and their circumstances were tenuous at best. She was in his employ. He couldn't make love to her and then demand that she inspect his linens and crockery and oversee the sweeping of his bloody floors.

No, they needed time. Needed to make sense of what they were to each other, what they could be. He couldn't afford to get swept up in desire. Not when so much was at stake for the both of them.

But that didn't stop him from continuing to kiss her. It merely kept him from taking what he wanted. It kept him from sliding inside her and claiming her as his. Instead, he licked into the honeyed recesses of her mouth, feasting on her as he had been longing to do from the moment he had first set eyes upon her. And she was kissing him back with a fierceness that all but brought him to his knees. It wasn't expertise so much as carnal need. This woman who had seen him at his worst, who had born his anger with such grace,

THE DUKE WHO DESPISED CHRISTMAS

whose determination had roused him from his self-imposed banishment.

She was a marvel, this woman.

Kissing him so sweetly, with wild abandon. Threading her fingers through his hair. He inhaled deeply of her scent, that floral, delicate soap that seemed so at odds with a woman of her profession and yet somehow felt at home on her. He wanted to wrap her in his arms and never let her go. To kiss her and kiss her and kiss her.

To—

Knock, knock, knock.

"Your Grace?"

Dunreave's voice was on the other side of the door, the equivalent of a pail of icy water being dumped over the two of them. Quint and Joceline broke apart, their breaths ragged.

He was reluctant to let her go just yet. This was too new. Too wonderful. Her mouth was lush and bruised from his kisses. Her eyes were dark with desire, her black lashes low. A spirited curl had come free of her coiffure to rest against her cheek, and he instinctively tucked it behind her ear. She was so beautiful, it hurt to look at her.

"Pardon me, Your Grace," Dunreave called again, more loudly this time. "Have you seen Mrs. Yorke? The household is in search of her as the dowager duchess has just arrived with her guests."

Quint took a step backward at the telling note of pinched censure in his butler's voice and the news that his mother was here as well. Dunreave knew damned well where Joceline was, and that was the reason he was politely knocking at the library door. *Damnation.* Quint had no wish to cause trouble for her.

Joceline's eyes went wide, and she leapt from the table

with a metallic jingle of her chatelaine, shaking out her skirts. Quint cleared his throat.

"Mrs. Yorke was just helping me with a small matter of grave import," he called to his butler. "She will join you forthwith." He frowned as the rest of the news Dunreave had imparted belatedly occurred to him. "Guests, did you say, Dunreave?"

"Yes, Your Grace. The Earl of Dreighton and his daughter, the Lady Diana Collingham."

Good God, why had his mother brought the earl and his daughter along with her? Surely she must know that the last thing in the world he would have wished for was unexpected guests.

Poor Joceline looked stricken. Blast it, this was not what he had intended when he had called her to the library. None of it was.

"Thank you for the clarification, Dunreave," he said loudly. "I'll need just another few moments with Mrs. Yorke."

"Of course, Your Grace," his butler intoned, still distant and disapproving.

"I'll go, Your Grace," she murmured, eyes lowering to the mess he'd made of the floor. "I'll see to it that a chambermaid cleans up this disarray."

"Joceline," he implored, keeping his voice low so that it wouldn't carry to Dunreave on the other side of the door, hating the formality that had returned to her demeanor and speech. "Don't go like this. Not yet."

"But I must," she countered, unsmiling. "I am your housekeeper, and your mother has just arrived from the train station. How would it look if I were to linger here with you a moment more, behind closed doors?"

Bloody hell, she was right, and he didn't like it. Not one whit.

"I'll want to speak with you later," he said. "We need to talk about this…about what we are."

"It's simple enough to me, Your Grace," she returned quietly, a sad smile on the lips he had just kissed so voraciously. "I am your servant, and you are my employer. We do not belong to the same world, and it can never be more than what we just shared. Even that was unwise. I never should have been so bold. It cannot happen again."

This was not what he wanted to hear. Nor would he accept it. Now that he knew Joceline was as drawn to him as he was to her, and now that he'd had her mouth on his, now that he knew how she tasted, the soft sounds of desire she made, the way her tongue writhed against his, he could not pretend none of it had happened. Nor could he pretend that he didn't want more.

"This isn't the end of what's between us, and you know it as well as I do," he said, needing to hear her confirm it.

But Joceline remained stoic, her housekeeper's mask firmly in place as she curtseyed as if they hadn't just nearly made love on his library table. "I'm afraid that it must be. If you'll excuse me, Your Grace, I should see to Mr. Dunreave and your guests."

Frustrated, he watched her run from him for the second time in as many days, knowing there was nothing he could do, thanks to his mother's arrival with unexpected guests. He couldn't very well carry on a clandestine affair with his housekeeper whilst Lord Dreighton, Lady Diana, and his own mother were in residence. To do so would only shame Joceline and his mother both.

No, he would have to wait. To bide his time.

And to find a way to get Joceline alone again without fear of interruption.

"Mrs. Yorke." Mr. Dunreave was stern and unsmiling as Joceline rushed to the butler's side in the corridor beyond the library.

She was all too aware of the sight she must present, mussed and flushed, her lips swollen from the duke's kisses. And she was also painfully cognizant of the fact that Mr. Dunreave knew she had been alone with Sedgewick in his library and just how long she had been there. He was a wise man, not easily fooled.

"Forgive me for being absent when the dowager arrived," she apologized. "I was distracted by some final preparations for the Christmas dinner that His Grace wished to discuss."

The blatant lie felt wrong, her cheeks heating beneath the butler's cold regard.

"The maids and footmen are overseeing the trunks and the unpacking for His Grace's guests," Mr. Dunreave said. "They have all been escorted to the drawing room for tea and cakes. I've taken the liberty of having Mary oversee the opening of two additional chambers for Lord Dreighton and Lady Diana."

The pointed tone and his critical stare, coupled with all the actions he had taken on her behalf, told her that the butler was quite put out with her.

"Thank you for attending to those matters for me," she said. "I'll go and speak with Mary now to make certain she has all the assistance she requires."

"I rather think it would be prudent for you to come with me instead, Mrs. Yorke. Some tea in your room would be just the thing."

As the housekeeper, her authority within the household was second only to the butler's. And despite her passionate embrace with the duke not long before, Joceline was pragmatic. She knew that there was no future for herself and a duke. She needed to keep the peace between herself and Mr.

Dunreave if she valued her position, which she very much did.

She needed this situation. It was the most lucrative position she'd had yet, and Mama and the children certainly needed the funds she was earning here quite badly.

"Of course, Mr. Dunreave," she allowed, pinning a false smile to her lips. "Some tea would be lovely."

They made their way to the servants' stair and descended into the maze of passageways beneath Blackwell Abbey, emerging at her room, where the fire was cheerfully burning, thanks to the still-room maid, and a pot of tea was at the ready. The silence that had fallen only served to heighten Joceline's ever-growing worry as they seated themselves in the small parlor area fashioned for such meetings and she served the butler his tea.

"How old are you, Mrs. Yorke?" Mr. Dunreave asked at last.

The question over her age nettled; the butler was not the first member of a household where she had been in service to question how a woman of her tender age had managed to so quickly work her way to lofty positions. Nor, she knew, would he be the last.

"I fail to see why my age should concern you, sir," she said politely. "Nor can I imagine that you called this interview with me merely to discuss how old I am."

"You are a clever woman to be sure, Mrs. Yorke." He sipped calmly at his tea, unperturbed. "Clever enough to know why the question might be asked of you, I've no doubt."

She stiffened, her spine going straight. "Mr. Dunreave, if you are implying that I am too young for the role of housekeeper, I can assure you that my age is immaterial."

Joceline took her duties seriously. It was largely a thankless role she played—and certainly an exhausting one.

But it was the best position in any household for a woman. Well, that wasn't precisely true. The best position in any household was wife. That grand title, however, wasn't achievable for someone like her, who had devoted her life to service.

"That was not what I was asking, Mrs. Yorke."

Her stomach tightened, dread coursing through her. For if the butler hadn't been suggesting she was too young to fulfill her duties, then she knew what he had been saying, and it was an even greater insult.

"I am afraid you will have to enlighten me," she told him coolly.

"Your age matters because I've never known a housekeeper as young as you appear to be, and one can only find oneself wondering at the reason. Why should Mrs. Joceline Yorke, above all other housekeepers in England, have found herself in the most powerful position in a household at such a youthful age?"

"I am five-and-twenty," she defended herself tightly. "I would hardly deem that youthful, nor so extraordinary a feat to become a housekeeper at my age."

Mr. Dunreave took another calm sip of his tea. "Tell me, Mrs. Yorke, did you closet yourself alone with the master of the last household where you were employed?"

And there it was, the ugly, raw implications the butler was making against her. Even worse, he was partially correct. She *had* been inappropriate and scandalous with the Duke of Sedgewick—she must not think of him as Quint ever again— but she had never previously conducted herself thus with another master of the house. Indeed, aside from the furtive loss of her innocence with a handsome footman when she had been younger and more naïve, she had taken immense care to be above reproach at all times.

It rankled that the butler would suggest she had risen to

the role of housekeeper through any means other than her own determination and hard work.

"No, Mr. Dunreave," she said with cool firmness, holding his stare even as every part of her vibrated with indignant fury. "I have never previously closeted myself alone with the master of the house. And nor, I may add, did I do so today. I merely answered His Grace's summons. He wished to speak about the Christmas menu, as I already told you."

"For over an hour? My, His Grace certainly did have a fair amount to say on the topic of plum pudding and mince pies."

The censure in Mr. Dunreave's countenance and his tone were both undeniable.

Over an hour? It was difficult to believe she had been ensconced in the library with the duke for that long. But perhaps it was true. She certainly had been lost in him, particularly when they had begun kissing. It had been as if all time had ceased to exist. As if there was nothing and no one but him. She had never known anything like it, and she had an instinctive feeling to her core that she never again would.

She forced a smile. "I suppose he is rather opinionated on the matter."

"And yet, His Grace has not taken an interest in the menu in two years," the butler observed.

"Mr. Dunreave, is there something you wish to say?" she demanded, losing her patience. "If so, I wish you would do so."

"There is indeed, madam," he told her, frowning. "When you arrived, I did my utmost not to judge your youth and beauty, nor to assume you had attained your position as housekeeper by making yourself improperly familiar with the masters of the houses where you served. However, I have witnessed far too much to remain silent about my suspicions. I feel it is imperative to warn you that if you wish to remain here at Blackwell Abbey, you would be wise to stay far, far away from His Grace. The duke has endured more suffering in his life than most, and he does not deserve to be lured by the wiles of a Siren."

Well, she thought. At least he had finally spoken plainly. It certainly explained his guarded nature where she was concerned. He had always been politely aloof, occasionally looking at her as if she might be hoping to filch some of the silver when he was sleeping. It hadn't been the silver that had concerned him after all. It was the Duke of Sedgewick.

She gripped her tea so tightly that she feared her cup might break, trying to keep her unruly emotions in check. "You have my word that I do not have any intention of luring His Grace, and I most certainly am no Siren, nor do I have wiles. But let us be perfectly clear. Are you threatening my livelihood, Mr. Dunreave?"

"I need not threaten your position at all," he bit out. "The dowager duchess is a woman of iron principle. When Her Grace discovers you have been acting the slattern with His Grace, she will dismiss you herself."

Heat rose to her cheeks, because again, the butler was not wrong. She had been the one to kiss Sedgewick. She had wrapped her arms around his neck and pressed herself shamelessly against him. And she had wanted far more from him than mere kisses. However, it hadn't been to gain any sort of favor. What she felt for him was honest and true. She couldn't defend herself with such a decree, however. If she confessed to what had occurred in the library, Mr. Dunreave would see her summarily tossed out on her ear, with nowhere to stay and no hope of finding a new situation.

"I can assure you, sir, that I will conduct myself with nothing less than the utmost of honor and dignity. I have no designs upon His Grace."

"See that you do, madam," Mr. Dunreave said gravely. "I am a lenient man, and I am willing to give you a final chance.

However, if there is the slightest hint of impropriety between yourself and the duke, I will be left with no choice other than to inform Her Grace of my suspicions. I can assure you that however much sway you may think to hold over the Duke of Sedgewick, Her Grace holds far more. She will see you gone in the blink of an eye. Do you understand me, Mrs. Yorke?"

"I understand you perfectly, Mr. Dunreave," she returned with what dignity she could muster. "If you will excuse me, I shall leave you to enjoy the remainder of your tea. There are a great many matters requiring my attention."

Without awaiting his response, she took her leave, fear warring with outrage. It was as she had known when she had walked into the library earlier, what she had known when she had kissed the duke, and it was the tenet that had guided her these last nine years of service. She did not belong to the charmed world of the aristocracy, and she never would. She was a servant, bound by the strict code of rules that governed her conduct.

And she would need to stay far, far away from the Duke of Sedgewick.

The lives of her mother and her siblings depended upon her, and she couldn't afford to risk their futures over whatever fleeting fancy the duke might feel for her. In the end, dukes didn't marry housekeepers. Just as she had been nearly decimated by the disappointment she'd suffered upon realizing she wouldn't have her Season with her aunt, she would only be crushed when the duke slaked his lust and had his fill. It was the age-old warning every woman in service knew by heart.

One could never dare to reach above one's station. Because when the inevitable fall came, it was impossible to survive.

CHAPTER 8

Quint was still reeling from the scorching kisses he'd shared with Joceline when his mother joined him in his study. He'd abandoned the library after righting the table as best as he could, leaving the broken glass to the dutiful efforts of a chambermaid who had arrived to discreetly whisk away the lingering evidence of his sins. Of course, the girl hadn't known what the reason was for the broken glass, nor was it her place to ask. But he had not been without guilt as he fled the scene of his crime, nor did he think he would ever be able to look upon that table again without recalling Joceline seated upon it, emerald eyes burning with passion, her lips dark and swollen from his kisses.

"My darling Sedgewick," the dowager duchess greeted, enveloping him in a perfumed embrace that didn't feel entirely genuine.

But then, that was how his every interaction with his mother had always been. He returned her embrace, narrowly avoiding being poked in the eye by the silk flowers and feathers adorning her extraordinarily high coiffure. His mother had forever been of the opinion that her lack of height could be countered by elaborate hair stylings. Once, to his utter horror, she had worn an entire family of stuffed birds in her hair for a ball. He'd spent the evening trying to avoid the glossy eyes of the wretched wrens, whose feathers had been dyed to match her purple silk.

"Mother," he said stiffly, patting her back.

Their relationship had never been particularly close. She had been aloof in his childhood, content to allow him to be raised by servants and then later to send him away to school. His father had been no better. The Duke of Sedgewick had been fifteen years his mother's senior, an austere, white-haired gentleman who had guarded his smiles and praise as if giving them would lessen his massive fortune. It had not been until Amelia had come into Quint's life—ironically enough, in a match made by their parents—that he had begun to understand what love truly was.

"Your hair." Mother extricated herself from his embrace and drew her shoulders back, frowning as she surveyed his appearance. "My heavens, Sedgewick, you look like Robinson Crusoe, stranded on a desert isle. It will need to be cut, of course. I cannot think your valet allows you to carry on this way."

Until recently, he hadn't one. He'd had Dunreave, who served as both butler and valet. Now, he had one of the footmen to assist him in shaving. But the lad hadn't dared to speak a word against Quint's hair, too wide-eyed from his movement up the service ladder.

"I'm not cutting my hair," he informed her.

"And whatever are you wearing?" she asked quite as if he hadn't spoken, her nose wrinkled as she took in the rest of him. "Where is your coat, and why are you wearing so much country tweed? I understand that you are here in the wilds of the north, but surely you have something more elegant to wear."

He frowned down at her. "I am wearing what I wish to wear."

She was still exhibiting a moue of distaste, her eyes returning to his hair as if it were a tragedy from which she couldn't look away. "Fortunately, I have brought some garments up from London. I sent word to your tailor, and he was exceptionally pleased to send along a selection of coats, waistcoats, and trousers. I directed Dunreave to take them to your rooms."

It was as if he hadn't said a word. His mother was holding a conversation entirely with herself, making sweeping decisions as if he hadn't the right to object. Why had he expected differently? This had been the way of it between them, his mother's overbearing nature trampling over any objections in her way. It was one of the reasons he had buried himself away here at Blackwell Abbey. She'd had the audacity to suggest but a few days after Amelia's funeral that when his period of mourning was over, he would need to begin looking for a new wife to breed so that he might carry on the line.

"…and you must really take better care with your appearance for Lady Diana's sake, if for no other reason. She is considered one of the greatest beauties in Polite Society, you know. She could have her choice of any husband."

His mother's continued prattling sifted through Quint's thoughts, making him snap back to attention. "What do Lady Diana's marital prospects have to do with what I wear or whether I cut my hair, Mother?"

Suspicion curdled his gut. He ought to have known his mother hadn't simply wanted to visit him for Christmastide. That the housekeepers she had sent him were her means of orchestrating some larger plan. That she would never be content to allow him to exist in peace.

"Nothing at all if you want to remain a bachelor hiding away in Durham, of course, and if you wish to allow some distant country cousin to become the next Duke of Sedgewick," she said pointedly, her tone suitably dramatic.

"We have discussed this, Mother," he reminded her tightly, clenching and unclenching his gloved hands at his sides.

"You have a duty to the title," she insisted. "You cannot simply molder away here with this ancient estate. You must think of your obligations."

"Is that why you have come, madam?" he demanded. "To remind me of my obligations?"

She heaved a sigh, the plumes in her silvery hair quivering. "It has been two years, Sedgewick. You are five-and-thirty. You must make another match, and you must beget an heir. To say nothing of Sedgewick Hall, which you have abandoned, and your many other duties."

He flexed his hands again, feeling the tightness of his ruined flesh, the heaviness in his chest as if the weight of that flaming beam had fallen upon him anew. "You needn't remind me of how much time has passed since my wife and child died."

"Apparently, I must. The proper period of mourning is six months. A year, at most. And yet, here you remain, buried in the north for two whole years, just as surely as if you lay down in her grave alongside her," she snapped.

Her callous words brought back memories he had valiantly sought to suppress. The sound of dirt falling on the coffin bearing what had remained of his wife and babe. The finality of the shovel striking earth. It was all returning to him now, the past at war with the present.

"I'll mourn as I see fit," he said, his tone harsh, but he didn't care. "You have no right to meddle in my affairs."

"I have no right?" She had the temerity to look affronted, a small, disbelieving laugh slipping from her. "Sedgewick, I am your mother. It is my solemn duty to remind you of yours."

He didn't want to think about duty or the pain of the past. All he wanted to think about right now was Joceline. He wanted—needed—to know what was between them. He wanted to see her again, kiss her again, touch her again. To be alone with her. She was *all* he wanted, full stop. But not only did they have the complication of their disparate stations, now they also had his mother, Lord Dreighton, and Lady Diana.

He passed a hand over his jaw, grim. "I'm more than aware of what is expected of me. I don't need you to remind me."

"Of course you do, Sedgewick." His mother fluttered nearer, venturing a consoling pat on his upper arm. "I was heartened when you didn't send the latest housekeeper I sent you away. It gave me hope that you're ready to return to your rightful place in society."

He didn't wish to speak about Joceline with his mother. Nor did he want the reminder that she was his housekeeper.

"Mrs. Yorke is remarkably adept at her position," he said politely, doing his utmost to expunge every hint of emotion from his voice.

It wouldn't do for Mother to suspect there was something between himself and Joceline that went beyond employer and domestic.

Another light pat, as if he were one of his mother's prized pugs gathered at her feet. "That is why I chose her. It's my most fervent hope that you will come to your senses in other areas as well, not just the running of your household. Give Lady Diana a chance. She would make you an excellent wife."

Good God.

It was as he'd thought. His mother was playing matchmaker. But he had no desire to be matched, damn it.

"I'm not interested in Lady Diana," he gritted.

"But you have yet to even meet her, darling." His mother smiled brightly. "She is a lovely young lady, and she was born and bred to be a duchess. She would do you great credit, you shall see."

His mother was, as ever, equal parts stubborn and persistent. He knew better than to continue arguing. It would garner him nothing but more frustration.

He forced a tight smile. "I'm sure you must be exhausted after your travels. Why don't you take a nap before dinner, Mother? Mrs. Yorke no doubt has had your chamber readied for you."

She beamed, unaware that he only made the overture so that she might go away and grant him some peace. "That is thoughtful of you, Sedgewick dear. I do believe I shall go and have a small lie-down before dinner. Until later, my darling son."

"Until later, Mother."

Mercifully, she took her leave, but he knew he wasn't to have a respite for long. Dinner loomed, far too soon. But first, there remained a flickering hope of catching Joceline alone between now and then.

～

JOCELINE BUSTLED TOWARD THE SERVANTS' stair when the door to the small salon nearest it opened, revealing the Duke of Sedgewick standing on the threshold. Silently, he gestured for her to join him. Her heart leapt in her throat as she cast a frantic glance about her, Mr. Dunreave's warnings still lying heavy as a boulder on her chest. No one was in sight, so with a sigh, she slipped into the salon with him, closing the door smartly at her back.

"Your Grace," she began, "what is it you want from me? Dinner is soon set to begin, and I have many tasks awaiting me."

He towered over her, his impressive height all the more pronounced in his black evening attire. He had dressed for dinner, she realized, a white neckcloth tied at his throat. She'd thought him handsome before, but the Duke of Sedgewick in formal blacks was enough to induce her to swoon.

"I wanted to speak to you," he said urgently, his blue-green gaze settling on her mouth.

She licked her lips, remembering the wondrous sensation of his sullen mouth on hers, so tender and possessive, and then banishing the yearning that rose up within her. She couldn't allow herself to fall back into his arms. Couldn't allow herself to linger here with him, where temptation beckoned and she could touch him again with such ease.

"Does it concern the running of the household?" she dared to ask, forcing herself to be stern with him.

"You know it doesn't."

She spun away, moving toward the door. "Then I'm afraid I must—"

His hand on her elbow stopped her.

"Stay," he begged, the raw emotion in his plea making her turn back to him.

What she saw reflected on his countenance—the naked yearning, the hunger that had sparked to life deep within her as well—tested her ability to resist him.

"Your Grace, your mother is in residence," she protested,

"along with guests. It is most improper for me to linger here with you."

"To the devil with propriety." He slid his hand down her forearm in a maddening caress, his leather-clad fingers finding hers as their palms connected. "You are my housekeeper. I can speak with you whenever I want."

"Mr. Dunreave is already suspicious," she forced herself to say. "I dare not risk being seen leaving the same room as you so soon after what happened earlier today."

"What was it that happened, Joceline?" he asked, his voice low and soft as velvet.

She inhaled sharply against a rush of desire. "I spent far too much time with you in the library and missed the arrival of the dowager duchess, the earl, and Lady Diana. That is what happened."

"No." He shook his head, his fingers tightening on hers. "It was far more than that. Admit it. Say it aloud."

He was so close, his scent wrapping around her. His gaze was on her lips, and she was remembering every moment of his passionate kisses, his hot tongue in her mouth. His own lips had parted, and he was breathing raggedly, as if it required every bit of strength he possessed to keep from devouring her again as he had on the library table. She swayed toward him, her skirts gliding against his trousers, her chatelaine tinkling.

"I cannot," she whispered, dangerously close to the precipice already, from nothing more than his proximity and her hand in his. "*We* cannot."

But the duke was determined. He caught her chin in his other hand, his hold firm but tender, his thumb tracing the slight dimple there.

"I've been thinking of nothing but you from the moment you left my side," he murmured.

"Your Grace," she protested, her voice as weak as her defenses.

For even as she tried to summon the faces of her mother and her younger siblings, all she could see was the way the Duke of Sedgewick was looking at her now, as if he wanted to take her in his arms and carry her away.

"Tell me you've not been doing the same," he challenged, his thumb trailing along the edge of her bottom lip.

A whimper escaped her. He was too much. How was she to resist him when he was setting her aflame? When he was handsome and vulnerable, when his eyes were slumberous with desire and the promise of so much more? She wasn't strong enough. She couldn't do it.

"Tell me to kiss you, Joceline."

Her eyes fluttered closed, trying to shut him out. Perhaps she could summon her defenses if she couldn't see his face, stark with an intoxicating blend of hunger and tenderness.

"I can't," she said, even as every part of her longed to say the words.

"I won't kiss you until you tell me you want it too," he murmured, moving his thumb along the bow of her upper lip now.

His touch swept over the seam of her lips, and a cry tore from her, because she couldn't bear another moment of denying him. Her eyes flew open, their stares melding. His head was bent toward hers, his dark-gold hair falling around the sharp angles of his face.

"I want it," she admitted quietly. "I want it too."

His hand moved to cup her cheek, and then his mouth was on hers, triumphant, demanding. His tongue slid deep, and low in her belly, a warmth unfurled. They kissed as if they were starved for each other. As if each press of their lips would be the last, tongues writhing, mouths open and voracious.

Their hands remained entwined, and he drew hers between them, flattening her palm over his heart so that she could feel his heat seeping into her, the frantic pace beating. His coat was smooth and fine, his chest a wall of muscle, and oh, the freedom to touch him—a wondrous gift. Her other hand settled on his shoulder as their lips moved as one. But that wasn't enough. She wanted to feel more of him. Wanted to know if his hair was as soft and smooth as it looked. So she slid her fingers along the rigid blade of his shoulder, then higher to his neck, and higher still, grasping a handful of his sleek hair.

He groaned and broke the kiss, his teeth nipping at her lower lip. The action was so carnal and animalistic, a far cry from the elegant, icy duke she had come to know. It was as if he sought to consume her. But she understood the feeling, because it was echoed deep within her. She wanted to tear off his clothes and see his scars. To run her lips over him, to lick him, to sink her teeth into him and leave a mark. She wanted him to be hers.

That can never be, said a voice inside her.

"I need to return before I'm missed," she forced herself to protest, even if the words felt sacrilegious after everything that had passed between them.

But she needed to remind herself of who she was, what she was. Needed to remind him, too. And the longer she tarried here in this salon, trading stolen kisses with him, the greater the peril for the both of them.

"Come to me tonight after everyone is abed," he murmured. "Come to my chamber. I'll be waiting for you."

His invitation shocked and intrigued her. The very notion of going to his bedroom was forbidden and yet so potently tempting that a rush of liquid need settled between her thighs, making her knees tremble.

"You know I cannot do that," she denied, even as she

wanted to more than she wanted anything. "If I were to be seen, it would be disastrous for the both of us."

Something flickered in his gaze, but then he kissed her again. Kissed her and kissed her until she forgot her objections. Until she forgot the past, the present, the future. Forgot anything that wasn't his mouth on hers, his body pressing into hers, insistent and masculine and so very big and strong.

When he ended the kiss, she was mindless and breathless, uncertain if she could even remain standing on her own two feet without clinging shamelessly to him for support.

He cupped her cheek, holding her captive in his unique stare, their lips a scant inch apart. "I need you longer, Joceline. I want you without worrying that we'll be interrupted."

The temptation was there, so very strong. She wanted to tell him *yes*. To throw caution to the wind and follow her heart instead of her head as she had these last nine years. And yet, she had far too many responsibilities, her younger siblings not old enough to earn their way, and her mother having no means of supporting them without abandoning them. She couldn't allow her brother and sisters to be torn apart. They depended upon her.

"I don't dare," she told him softly, sadly, wishing their circumstances were different. "The risk is far too great. I'm sorry, Your Grace."

Reluctantly, she forced herself to step away from him, the mantel clock chiming to tell her that she needed to go at once. They hadn't any time left.

"I'm sorry," she added, eyes welling with tears she blinked furiously away.

"Joceline," he implored again, looking as stricken as she felt. "Please."

Shaking her head, she moved swiftly from the room,

dabbing at her eyes with the back of her hand to remove all evidence of the emotions she couldn't allow herself to feel.

The Duke of Sedgewick was not for her, and there was no better confirmation of that than when she passed by Mr. Dunreave in the servants' hall, his gaze calculating and shimmering with new suspicion.

~

Lady Diana Collingham was a flaxen-haired beauty. A true English rose with a porcelain complexion, sky-blue eyes, and a rosebud mouth that seemed to be perpetually turned upward in a smug smile. And why shouldn't she be smug, Joceline thought crossly as she made her way to her small bedroom, feet aching to rival her back. She was young and unfailingly lovely, she was a fine lady, and she was dressed in the comeliest silk gowns Joceline had ever seen, confections that would have put her cousins to shame.

She was also hoping to become the next Duchess of Sedgewick.

The latter had been made as plain as the chapped, work-roughened skin on Joceline's hands after enduring three days of presiding over every meal and entertainment for the duke and his guests. True to her word, she had managed to keep her distance from him, playing her role flawlessly, leaving no room for Mr. Dunreave to find fault with her after her lapses of sanity in the salon and library.

She faced her duties with a new resolve, doing her utmost to contain the burning, agonizing jealousy that sliced through her whenever she found herself in the same room as the gorgeous Lady Diana. Because although she knew it was wrong and that it was certainly no fault of the lady's that their stations in life were so dissimilar, Joceline hated the constant reminder that she was the kind of woman a duke kissed secretly behind closed doors, but Lady Diana was the kind of woman a duke would marry.

And for his part, Sedgewick seemed to have accepted her denial of his overtures. No more furtive embraces in shadowy rooms. No more invitations to his bedroom. Instead, he was occupied by escorting Lady Diana about and by accompanying his mother. It was just as well, she had told herself, trying to ignore the deep sense of disappointment the realization inevitably caused.

At least she could be secure in her situation. No one would sack her. She could remain the housekeeper at least for a year, at which point the duke might be newly wed or about to marry, and she could collect her bounty. She would move on to a new position before the pain of watching Sedgewick take a wife and begin a family.

With a heavy sigh, she entered her darkened chamber, where the only light was from the small, flickering fire in the grate, closing the door behind her. And instantly noticed the large, undeniably masculine figure in the shadows.

A gasp tore from her.

"Hush," came Sedgewick's familiar voice, a low, decadent rumble that made her heart leap. "You have no notion how difficult it was for me to sneak into your chamber."

She pressed a hand over her wildly beating heart, trying to suppress the sheer joy that had risen within her at his presence, regardless of how wrong and dangerous it was. "Your Grace, you shouldn't be here."

He stood to his full height, towering over her, so tall that his head nearly reached the low ceiling of her room. "I know, but I had to find a way of seeing you since you didn't come to me, and I didn't want to risk during the day with the earl, my mother, and Lady Diana all underfoot."

His voice was quiet, and she was grateful that he was

THE DUKE WHO DESPISED CHRISTMAS

indeed taking care. But he was here, in her room! He had been sitting on her bed. If Mr. Dunreave were to find out…

"No one will sack you, Joceline," Sedgewick reassured her as if he could read her thoughts, moving to stand before her. "I promise you that. You needn't fear for your position."

She wetted her lips. "But Mr. Dunreave—"

"Is also in my employ," he interrupted firmly. "I understand your trepidation where your character is concerned, but please know you may be my housekeeper until you choose otherwise."

His words did somewhat assuage her fear that Mr. Dunreave would see her sacked. However, his presence in her bedroom was still forbidden.

"Thank you," she said softly. "But you must go. You cannot be in my private room."

"Do you want me to go?" he asked.

She closed her eyes for a moment, blotting out the sight of him, but it didn't aid her ability to resist him this time any more than the last. "Your Grace…"

"Quint," he murmured. "When we are alone, I would have you call me Quint."

It wasn't the first time he had offered the invitation, of course. But she had been forcing herself to think of him as the Duke of Sedgewick, regardless of the intimacy he so temptingly offered.

She opened her eyes again to find him looking down at her with such naked yearning that an ache sprang forth deep within her. "You know I can't. Allowing familiarity between us is foolish."

"Is it?" He took her hands in his, and she allowed it, wanting his touch even as she knew she shouldn't. "Why is it foolish? Tell me."

"You know why. Because you are a duke, and I am your servant. It is simply not done."

"I don't care about what society thinks is proper."

"As a duke, you have that liberty," she reminded him. "As a housekeeper, I do not."

"I don't think I ever despised the shackles my title places upon me, at least not truly. Not until now."

They stared at each other, silent meaning passing between them, hunger sparking to life, dangerous and heady. The illicit nature of their meeting, the shadows in her room, the flickering fire, the small quarters—all contributed to cast a sensual spell over her.

"What do you want from me?" she asked, desperate to keep these unwanted feelings at bay, to resist him.

"I want…" His words trailed off for a moment as his gaze devoured her face. "I want to court you."

A hysterical laugh bubbled up from within her. "You cannot court your housekeeper."

"Why not?"

"Because I don't belong to your world. Because I have too many duties awaiting me, and I must attend your household and guests. Because you are meant to court a beautiful aristocrat like Lady Diana."

She could have gone on listing reasons, but she stopped herself, for her emotions were running too high, like the waters of a rain-swelled stream threatening to flood its banks.

"Joceline." He brought her hands up, kissing her knuckles, which ached from stoning raisins and pounding lump sugar earlier that evening. "Please allow me to explain myself, if I may."

How could she deny him when he was so vulnerable before her? His expression was earnest, and he clung to her fingers as if she were the rarest, most precious treasure he had ever beheld. He was still wearing his evening finery from dinner, cutting an elegant figure. For a wild moment, she wished that she had been seated with him at the dining table. That they had conversed and flirted and she had worn something suitably lovely, a silk evening gown trimmed with flowers instead of a gray woolen frock covered with an apron.

"Go on," she allowed against her better judgment, for she knew the longer she allowed him to remain here in her space, the harder it would be for her to fight against her intense attraction to him.

"I don't want to court Lady Diana. I don't want anyone but you." He paused, shaking his head as if he were perplexed, trying to sift his thoughts together into some semblance of order. "I never expected to feel this way. It confounds me and astounds me, but I cannot help it. You are all I can think about. When I wake up, I cannot wait to see you."

"Please," she interjected, not certain if she could bear to hear more, for it was everything she had secretly yearned to hear. "You needn't say more."

"But I do need," he insisted, squeezing her fingers gently. "Do you not see? I am nothing but raw, aching need, and the fault is yours. I spend all day hoping for a fleeting sight of you, for a shared glance. I go to sleep at night thinking of you, imagining your glorious black hair unbound, wondering if it's as soft and silken as I think it is. I didn't want this. I didn't ask for it."

The vehemence of his tone cut away at her defenses.

"I didn't want it either," she protested. "Nor did I ask for it. I came to Blackwell Abbey to be your housekeeper, that is all."

And a part of her was begging him to allow her to continue to be nothing more than just his servant, that part of Joceline that was mired in obligation. The part that had been diligently working to send everything she could home.

But the rest of her—the selfish, longing, foolish part of her—needed to hear him acknowledge what he felt. To hear the full extent of how strongly he was drawn to her. Because she felt the same relentless pull.

"But you are far more than that now, Joceline," he said, his voice low and beseeching. "Do you not see? I have spent these last few weeks fighting it with all I have. Denying what I feel. I was perfectly content in my misery—or at least, I thought I was. But then you came here with your sunny smiles and your stunning cheek, and your garlands and your bloody trees. You unlocked a part of me I thought was gone, brought it back to the light, and I don't know how to be this man again, a man who can find happiness and hope after so much loss and grief. I don't know what it means, what I feel for you. All I know is that I think I'm in lo—"

"No," she cried out, interrupting his declaration before he could complete it, for it was too painful. She wanted it too much, with a desperation that terrified her. She couldn't have it.

But that was immaterial. For now, she would seize what she could.

Joceline threw herself at him. Into him. Their bodies collided as she rose to her toes and pressed her mouth over his, kissing him, showing him what she didn't dare to acknowledge with words. Because quite suddenly, it didn't matter what would happen tomorrow. It didn't matter that she was a servant in his employ and he was a wealthy duke who was far above her station. It didn't even matter if she had to find a different situation for herself.

She had fallen in love with the Duke of Sedgewick.

She loved this beautiful, broken, imperfect man who had suffered unimaginable loss and tragedy. And she intended to show him just how much, even if tonight was all she could ever have with him.

Their entwined hands came apart, hers settling on his broad chest, his on her waist. Their kisses were frantic and deep, hard and hot. She quickly grew impatient, needing more. She glided her fingers under his coat, helping him to shrug out of it. The garment slid to the floor with a whisper of sound as she settled on the buttons of his waistcoat. And even though her hands were tired and sore from her tasks that day, she worked those buttons out of their moorings with absurd, unerring haste, stripping him of that boundary as well as she opened for his questing tongue.

She was not the only one exploring, caressing. His fingers found the fastening of her chatelaine, but when she felt him fumbling, she broke the kiss. "Allow me."

Joceline made short work of removing the pin holding it in place at her waist, laying it carefully upon a tabletop for tomorrow's use, her heart giving a pang at the thought that their time together would be so brief.

"My gloves," he murmured, flexing his fingers before him, staring at the leather coverings he still donned to shield his scars from others.

"Will you remove them for me?" she asked gently.

He hesitated, indecision flashing on his handsome face.

"I saw your hands before," she reminded him. "But if you prefer to keep them on, I understand."

"No." A muscle tensed in his wide jaw. "I want to feel you."

The sweet thrill of anticipation went through her, an ache pulsing to life between her thighs. "Yes."

She watched as he stripped them off himself, revealing the puckered skin on his big hands, his fingers long and thick. To her, the scars were a symbol of his honor. The reminder that he had fought so valiantly to save the woman he loved. And Joceline loved him all the more for it.

She took his hands in hers, and, as he had done earlier, brought them to her lips.

"You needn't—"

His protest died as she kissed his hands, his knuckles, his fingertips, then turned them over, kissing his scarred palms as well.

"Joceline." His voice was soft as velvet and smooth as silk, filled with so much raw need that it made liquid desire pool low in her belly.

She kissed him some more, and then when she was breathless with longing, she brought his hands to her breasts, pressing them to her bodice, where, beneath the shield of her corset, her nipples were hard and almost painfully sensitive.

"Will you undress me, Quint?" she asked, allowing herself the freedom of using his given name.

He lowered his head and seized her lips as he found the fastening of her simple bodice, opening it as he kissed her. There had always been an efficient economy in removing her garments for Joceline. The movements served a purpose. The quicker they were done, the sooner she could go to sleep and rest for the new day and all its waiting work. But there was such heady, potent luxury in having Quint undress her. She wanted it to go on forever, his caresses moving over tapes and buttons and hooks. But she also wanted it to end swiftly so that she could feel his skin on hers.

Remembering that she was not the only one who needed her clothing undone, she returned to his neckcloth, her tongue tangling with his as she tugged at the knot and pulled the linen free. She stepped out of her skirts and petticoat, feeling the heavy fabric glide down her hips to pool around her booted feet on the floor.

He raised his head then, breathing as harshly as she was, his stare glinting with undisguised passion. "Sit on the bed."

She didn't understand his request, her wits too addled from his kisses and his hands on her. "Why?" she managed, confused.

"You are always tending to me," he explained, kissing her jaw, her nose, her cheek before straightening again. "It is my turn to tend to you."

Protest was ingrained in her. This beautiful duke should not be waiting upon her. But he folded her hand in his, and the delicious intimacy of his skin on hers overtook any need to object as he guided her the three steps to her narrow bed.

She sat on the edge, watching in bemusement as he sank to his knees before her and lifted her right foot, settling the sturdy sole on his thigh. With calm, efficient motions, he untied the laces, loosened her boot, and slid it off. She made a soft sound of pleasure, flexing her toes, and he rubbed her stockinged foot, somehow unerringly finding all the places that pained her and soothing them. She hoped he didn't notice the repairs she'd made to her stockings, nor the coarse, cheap quality of them. But if he did, he didn't comment upon it, his strong fingers expertly kneading her arch instead.

"How does that feel?" he asked.

"Heavenly," she admitted.

"Good." The smile he sent her was at once both boyish and wicked, dimples grooving his cheeks. "My God, you are so beautiful."

His praise warmed her, and though she knew she must look a far cry from the elegant Lady Diana in her simple drawers and stockings, her plain corset and chemise, her hair pinned away in the same easy chignon she twisted it into herself each morning, she *felt* beautiful.

She smiled back at him. "Thank you."

In truth, she thanked him for so much more than his tender ministrations on her foot. But emotions and yearning and rising desire robbed her of the ability to elucidate. So she simply watched as he moved to her left boot, untying the laces and pulling it free as well before rubbing this stockinged foot also.

"I've been thinking about doing this for days," he said, taking an ankle in each hand and rubbing her calves.

"You have?" She sighed with bliss as he found muscles she hadn't even known were tight and sore, tenderly working them into submission.

"Ever since you kissed me." He caressed higher, along her outer thighs, moving under her chemise as he went. "I wouldn't allow myself to think of it before then, for fear that you didn't feel what I do."

"I feel it too," she confessed, inhaling when he framed her hips and tugged her forward with a swift yank, almost pulling her completely from the bed.

He kissed her knee over the white cotton of her drawers, his fingers finding the buttons on her waistband and plucking them free. "I didn't dare to hope."

Her drawers loosened, and he pulled on them. She lifted her bottom to aid him in his efforts, the undergarments slipping free. Although her chemise remained in place about her knees, covering her modesty, her thighs pressed together, a new sense of intimacy fell over her. He was going to see her —all of her.

And she wanted him to.

What a sinner she was. Her garters came undone, first one, then the other, and he dragged each one slowly, deliciously, down her leg, and she no longer cared. Instead, she admired him, so powerful and elegant in his shirtsleeves and trousers, the firelight dancing off his dark-gold hair as it swept over his face while he finished his task.

Reaching behind her, she snagged the laces of her corset and pulled, untying this knot as well, for if she didn't soon loosen it, she feared she wouldn't be able to breathe. Her heart was pounding, her lungs struggling to keep up with the

THE DUKE WHO DESPISED CHRISTMAS

demands of her body. The stays sagged, giving her relief, and she undid the hooks and eyes at the busk with practiced ease.

The corset fell to the bed, leaving her in only her worn chemise, which she knew to be quite transparent from years of washing without replacing it. His gaze darkened, falling to the swells of her breasts, heavy and full, her nipples jutting toward him through the thin fabric.

With a groan, he moved closer, releasing his hold on her legs to cup the mounds of her breasts in his hands. His head dipped, and he took the aching peak of one into his mouth, sucking hard.

A small sound of pleasure tore from her before she could help herself, for she felt that delicious pull deep in her core. He kissed the curve of her breast and then moved to the other, suckling that one as well.

It was good, so good, but not enough. She wanted his mouth on her without cloth between them. Grasping handfuls of her chemise, she pulled it to her waist. The movement dislodged him from her breast, but he understood what she was doing, sensual approval on his face as he watched her pull the chemise from under her bottom and then lift it over her head.

"Forgive me," he murmured. "I was too eager."

"There's nothing to forgive."

She threw the undergarment over her shoulder, not caring where it went, and, holding his stare, reached for the hairpins keeping her unruly curls in submission. Heavy tendrils fell as she removed the pins, stacking them in her palm until she was finished and a curtain of hair fell down her back.

"Joceline." His voice was hoarse and raw, tinged with amazement and awe.

She'd never been naked like this with a man before, and she knew she ought to feel some need for modesty. That she should cover herself—or, at the very least, lie beneath the bedclothes and await him rather than to put her body on bold display. But the hungry look he gave her was all she needed to know he appreciated her boldness.

That and the way he insinuated himself between her thighs, nudging them apart, and with a sound of pure carnal delight, took her nipple in his mouth again. This time, she was rewarded with wet heat, the play of his tongue. She arched her back, offering herself to him, giving him so much more than just her body. Giving him her heart, herself, all that she had to give.

She ran her fingers through his hair, and he laved indecent attention upon first one breast, then the other.

"Quint," she whispered, the sound of her own breathing and the suction of his mouth joining the popping of the fire to make wicked music.

Every part of her was intensely aware, her senses almost painfully acute.

He moved back to her other breast. "So beautiful. More beautiful than I imagined."

She bit her lip to keep from making more noise, mesmerized by the sight of his handsome face nestled against her, his mouth on her nipple. She was melting. Mindless. His hands were in her hair, running through the strands with such reverence, as if they were fashioned of gold, his tongue flicking over the distended peak of her breast. And then he kissed a path of fire down her rib cage, his mouth finding the indentation of her navel, his hands guiding her legs farther apart, lips traveling lower still. Nothing could have prepared her for the kiss he pressed there, between her legs, in that most sensitive place of all.

Good heavens. His mouth was... He was... His tongue. His tongue?

Sweet God, his *tongue*.

He was devouring her as if she were a feast, lustily licking and kissing and sucking, spreading her folds with his thumbs, moaning into her, the vibration echoing in the bud of her sex.

A squeak emerged from her. She clapped a hand over her mouth. It was sinful. She was sure it was wrong, what he was doing, but she was also sure that nothing had ever felt as good, nor had any sin been more worthwhile, than the Duke of Sedgewick on his knees before her, face buried between her legs, tongue coaxing the sort of pleasure from her she'd never previously known existed.

She was embarrassingly wet between her legs, a state that was only heightened by his tongue, which was circling, licking, driving her ever closer to the edge of some dark and dangerous height. He licked lower, his tongue swirling over her entrance, then dipping inside, and her hips bucked when his thumb rolled over the small bundle that only she had ever teased. The poor footman hadn't known how to please a woman any more than she had known how to please a man.

The pleasure was wondrous. Impossible. His tongue glided deeper, in and out, as his thumb swirled. And the pleasure roared over her, fast and intense as a runaway locomotive on a track.

Her body seized, bliss ricocheting up and down her spine. She bit her palm to keep from screaming, wave after wave of ecstasy washing over her. And still, he was relentless, tonguing her, working her nub, until somehow his mouth had returned, and he was suckling as he had her breast, only this time it was the most secret part of her, and the tip of his finger traced over her seam, finding her channel with ease. He plunged into her effortlessly, the stretch a shock—it had been years for her since she had hastily coupled, scarcely even knowing what was happening, still fully clothed.

But this, oh this. It was glorious. A second finger joined

the first, probing, sliding in and out, then in deeper and deeper. Meanwhile, his mouth was locked on her bud, sucking sweetly, so sweetly, the sound of him taking his fill of her mingling with her ragged breaths. She felt the demanding pressure of his teeth then, in a place where she was particularly sensitive, timed with the drive of a third finger, and everything inside her shattered. She came with a strangled cry and a wet rush from her core, and as the bliss undulated through her ravished body, he kissed her inner thigh tenderly, his lips glistening with her desire.

"So sweet, Joceline," he said, dispelling any lingering hint of self-consciousness she might have been harboring. "You taste even better than I'd hoped."

His fingers were still inside her, stretching her, filling her. But that wasn't enough. Unlike that lone time from her past, she didn't wish the physical joining to end. There was no pain, only astonishing pleasure. His gaze was on her sex, watching, she thought, the way she gripped those fingers, her inner muscles still convulsing, though with less fury now than they originally had.

"Are you a virgin, Joceline?" he asked softly, those knowing fingers still pumping inside her, drawing more sensation from her when she thought it impossible there could be more.

"No," she answered honestly. "Many years ago, when I was young...I was foolish..."

It felt strange to speak of such matters when he was lodged inside her, and yet the pressure he was renewing deep within her was so glorious she didn't care. She thought that she might do anything he asked of her, answer any question, run naked about all of Blackwell Abbey if he but requested, just for more of this.

"Hush," he said, kissing her sex again, his fingers gliding free. "It doesn't matter other than that I'm quite desperate. I didn't want to hurt you." Another kiss, reverent, the swipe of his tongue over her highly sensitized bud.

"You won't hurt me," she promised, not even sure if it was true.

Last time, it had not been pleasant. Intervening years had fogged her memory. She'd forgotten the experience, the young man. It hadn't mattered—her life had been given to service. And it no longer mattered now. She didn't even care if Quint caused her pain. She just wanted him.

He stood abruptly, tearing at the fall of his trousers, and then his cock emerged, thick and long and ready. That part of him was untouched by flame, and much larger than the footman's had been. Much, much larger.

"Lie back on the bed, love," he said, his voice strained with tamped-down desire.

Love.

Oh, how that lone word felt, landing directly in her heart. If only it could be forever hers, if *he* could be forever hers. But there wasn't time to reflect upon that now. They needed to finish what they had begun.

She did as he bid, lying on the bed, her legs still dangling down the side, the position awkward. But then he took her ankles in a firm but gentle grasp, guiding her legs along his chest, and he pulled her bottom against him so that the ruddy head of his cock glanced over her folds.

"Are you ready?" he asked.

She stared up at him, thinking him so handsome, her brooding duke who had endured so much. Loving him.

"I'm ready," she said.

He moved, the cords in his neck standing in relief, and there was pressure at her entrance. A flex of his hips, and he was inside her, and filling her even fuller than his fingers had, so deep and so perfect. There was a twinge as her body adjusted to this new invasion, but when he moved, slowly at first, and then with faster, harder thrusts, he began stoking the flames of her pleasure once more. The angle, the sturdy feeling of him behind her legs, the sight of his handsome face tightened with pleasure as he made love to her—it was all so much.

She was weightless, a creature of pleasure rather than drudgery, and it was as if she were a phoenix in that moment on her small bed in the dark confines of her bedroom. No longer a housekeeper, but a goddess rising from the ashes. He murmured to her, his hands on her hips, pulling her into him, his thick shaft driving deep, then withdrawing, then driving deep again.

Joceline was perilously near to splintering apart. To crying out so that all the household could hear her, everyone above stairs and below. She caught a handful of bedclothes and pressed them over her mouth just in time for her body to fly apart again, her inner walls contracting on him as spasms of bliss rocketed through her. He groaned and hastened his pace, faster, harder, until he stiffened and surged deep, his cock pulsing inside her as the heat of his release jetted into her body.

As swiftly as he had entered her, he withdrew, somehow arranging her on the bed so that her head was on the pillow where it belonged and her legs no longer dangled over the edge. And then he joined her, folding his big body against hers on the tiny mattress, drawing her into his protective warmth.

It was in that moment that she realized he'd never fully removed his clothing and he was still wearing his shirt and trousers. She'd yet to see all his scars.

Carefully, she turned so that she faced him, and they lay nose-to-nose, their breaths mingling, lips dangerously close. She traced a finger down the line of buttons bisecting his shirt. "Will you show me?"

"Joceline," he began.

But she kissed him swiftly. "Please. I want to see you."

Clenching his jaw, he nodded. "Promise you won't run and hide when you see the monster you've just given yourself to?"

Oh, how her heart ached to hear him speak of himself thus.

She kissed him again before breaking away to stare earnestly into his eyes. "I know the man I've given myself to, and he's not a monster at all. He's brave and strong and good."

He cupped her cheek, his thumb stroking. "Sweet girl. I'm none of those things. I'm old and bitter and scarred."

"Not so old," she denied. "And I do believe my Christmas greenery has cured you of some of your bitterness." She kept her tone light and teasing, cherishing this newfound intimacy between them, so different from what had come before. "And as for your scars, they are what make you who you are."

And I love that man.

But these were words she kept to herself, for such a confession would reveal far more to him than she had with her mere body. And nothing had changed beyond the four walls of her small, shadowy room. He was still her employer. She was still his housekeeper. In the morning, she would rise to a new day of duties, and he would share breakfast with a glorious English rose eminently more suited to be his duchess.

She refused to allow any of that to ruin the time they had remaining.

"You're certain you wish to see me?" he asked, his tone hesitant, a far cry from the icy, sneering duke who had first greeted her at Blackwell Abbey weeks ago.

Now, he was Quint. *Her* Quint. Vulnerable and warm and wonderful, holding her in his arms.

"I'm certain," she told him without faltering.

He nodded, edging away from her slightly, for there wasn't much room on her narrow bed. His left hand went to the buttons at his throat, opening them slowly, his fingers struggling.

She moved to help him. "Let me."

He swallowed hard, and she tracked the movement of his Adam's apple, rising and falling, his body going still as he allowed her to pull each fastening from its mooring, one by one, until she had reached the waistband of his trousers, where his falls had been halfheartedly restored, his spent cock tucked away. A swath of his chest and lean abdomen were revealed to her, alternately smooth and puckered, leaving no doubt of the agony he must have suffered during his convalescence.

It was incredible he had survived at all, and that was plain to see, as was the place where the beam had fallen, almost neatly across his torso. She smoothed the twain ends of his shirt farther apart, revealing more of him. His flat male nipples had been largely unscathed, so too his collarbone and pectorals. But just beneath, the raised, red flesh that had been burned was there, a testament to the strength and bravery she'd told him he possessed.

"You see?" he said darkly. "A monster. I warned you."

"No." She kissed his chest. Lower. Moved down his body, her lips traveling over every bit of scarred flesh. "Never a monster." More kisses as he tensed and held still beneath her. "You are a beautiful man. *My* beautiful man."

The last few words were foolish, escaping her before she could think better of them, regardless of the fact that she felt them to her marrow. He could never truly be hers. But for this one night, he was.

THE DUKE WHO DESPISED CHRISTMAS

A breath hissed from him as she found his navel, which had been untouched by flame, and then she worked the buttons on his trousers, pulling them down his hips along with his drawers. He helped her, tearing them off and shrugging out of his shirt, finally as gloriously naked as she, his cock already erect and stiff again.

Feeling bold, she encircled him with her hand in a gentle grasp, reveling in the newness of his skin, soft and hot, yet his member so rigid beneath. An answering ache throbbed to life within her. She wanted him again. Where he was concerned, she was greedy. If this was to be the only time she had him to herself, in her bed, she intended to make the most of it. And she wanted to show him how she felt for him, how his scars only made her desire him—and love him—more.

⁓

QUINT HELD his breath as Joceline tentatively stroked his erect cock. Her touch was light, untutored. She might not have been a virgin, but it was apparent she hadn't a great deal of experience. Never mind. He would take great pleasure in teaching her.

He wrapped his hand around hers, showing her how to increase the pressure, moving her hand up and down his length, heedless of his scars. They didn't matter now. For the first time, they felt like they were a part of him rather than something that had happened to him. It had taken him two years to find this peaceful state of acceptance, along with the determination of one tenderhearted woman who hadn't allowed him to wallow in bitterness.

When she touched him, he felt whole again. When she kissed his scars without revulsion, her soft lips feathering over the ruined flesh, he felt only desire for her. Love for her, too. So much love.

He would tell her.

He would marry her.

She couldn't be his housekeeper any longer. Not after this. But he couldn't think properly with her hand on his shaft, which was thickening and longing for her again, moisture seeping from the slit in his crown. He had denied himself pleasure for so long, and rediscovering it with Joceline felt like nothing less than a miracle.

She felt like a miracle, too.

A miracle of inky hair and silken pink lips, of lush breasts and full hips and emerald eyes, of drab gowns and chatelaines, of mercy and understanding, of kindness and fortitude. A miracle somehow sent to him, his own Christmas gift. The best one he would ever receive.

"Like this?" she asked softly, her hand moving along his cock.

"Yes," he hissed on a groan. "Just like that, sweetheart."

He released her hand, allowing her to pleasure him at her own pace now, running his fingers through the thick, raven curls she kept pinned in her sensible chignons. Her glistening eyes met his, and she kissed his chest, her lips feathering over his hideous scars, healing every expanse of twisted skin she touched, a benediction.

For a few moments, he allowed himself the luxury of her mouth, her touch. Nothing more than his thudding heart, her questing lips, and her confident hand. Gratitude swept over him, mingling with all the other sensations, a rush so strong that it swelled inside his chest, making him catch his breath.

She paused over his heart, casting an inquisitive glance in his direction. "Is something wrong?"

"No," he told her thickly, cupping her nape and urging her toward him. "Everything is right. So very right."

He brought her lips to his and kissed her deeply, his tongue slipping inside the velvet heat of her mouth. She was sweet, so sweet. He could kiss her forever and never grow weary of it. What a blessing she was, this lively, clever woman. He might have known she would embrace her sensuality with the same pragmatism she applied to the managing of his household. Her tongue plundered his mouth in return, and she moaned softly with delight, her hand on him moving with increasing urgency.

If he didn't take care, he would spill before he was even inside her again.

He couldn't have that. Quint shifted her, breaking the kiss, positioning her so that she was astride him, the full, ripe globes of her breasts dangling in his face like a taunt. So he took one stiff nipple into his mouth and sucked, his fingers slipping into her folds to find her slick and wet. His seed leaked from her entrance, blending with her dew, and he found the combination of the two of them deeply rousing. He toyed with her cunny, painting the creamy spend over the petals of her sex and the swollen nub of her clitoris until she writhed, another small moan leaving her kiss-bruised lips.

Quint released her nipple, thinking how glorious she looked, glossy-eyed and beautiful, her pale skin bathed in the firelight's glow, her body curved and soft and womanly, her hair a midnight cloud spilling down her back and over her shoulders.

"Again?" he rasped, reminding himself that he had already made love to her with great abandon once and that he must consider her comfort.

But he needn't have worried. Joceline was tantalizing the head of his cock with her thumb, rocking against his hand, the fringe of her lashes low as she gave him a sultry look. "Again."

She didn't need to tell him twice.

Quint grasped her hips and lifted her, positioning her so that she was above his rudely protruding cock, which demanded more of her, all of her, without end. He wanted her to ride him. To take her pleasure.

But she hovered over him, an expression of adorable befuddlement on her face. A new position for her, then.

"Put my cock inside you," he told her.

She rose on her knees, shifting, her grasp on his cock still tight and wonderful. "Like this?"

She dragged the sensitive tip of him up and down her center, slicking him with the moisture seeping from her. It was the two of them, their pleasure, their desire, commingling and becoming one. And for a moment, he lost his breath, a bolt of lust and possession so crazed and potent tearing through him that he could do nothing, say nothing.

"Just like that," he managed tightly, struggling to control himself.

She slid his cock down her cleft, bringing the head of him to her center. Warm wetness bathed the tip, making him clench his jaw. Then she lowered herself onto him, taking all of him at once, and he was deep inside her again, surrounded by her heat and her tight channel, and he nearly shouted out victoriously to the rafters.

At the last moment, he recalled himself, settling for sucking her other nipple into his mouth instead. Her hands landed on his shoulders for purchase, and he kept his grip on her hips, guiding her into a pace that she quickly made her own. He couldn't keep himself from moving with her, meeting her thrust for thrust as he suckled both breasts, her hair fanning over them like a silken curtain.

Her pinnacle caught him by surprise, swift and sudden, her inner muscles clenching so tightly she nearly squeezed him from her. Holding her still, he rocked upward, into her, absorbing every ripple of her release, the slickness of her cunny taking him to the verge as well. She felt like heaven on earth, and he never wanted this to end.

She cried out more loudly than was safe, but he was too far gone to care if anyone overheard. Let the whole damned household come down upon them. He would declare himself to all the servants. To everyone who cared to listen. Because this woman—Joceline Yorke—was meant to be his.

Another thrust, and he lost himself inside her, the rush up his spine intense as fireworks unleashed across a dark sky. The pleasure was so exquisite that stars speckled his vision. Holding her tightly to him, Quint filled her with his spend, gasping her name into the night.

CHAPTER 9

It was Christmas Eve morning, and a thin coating of snow had painted the landscape an ethereal silver-white overnight. The reflection of the sun off the icy coating was almost unnatural as Quint descended the grand staircase to the great hall, where a large bank of windows overlooked the rolling parkland beyond.

The world was a new place. Quint was a new man. The future was suddenly filled with possibilities. And he was counting the minutes until he could have Joceline back in his arms where she belonged. All he had to do was navigate these rather unusual circumstances with prudence and a mind to avoid causing scandal.

He would not have Joceline hurt, nor would he allow any hint of gossip to spread about her. He was more than aware of the unusual nature of an aristocrat taking his housekeeper as his wife—in his set, such things simply were not done. Or, at least, they hadn't been until now. Which meant he needed to proceed with the plan he had begun to make as he had slipped from her room in the bowels of the night like a thief afraid of being caught and sent to the gallows.

THE DUKE WHO DESPISED CHRISTMAS

"Sedgewick!"

Startled from his thoughts, he glanced up to find his mother storming toward him in a flurry of navy silk, her countenance hard as marble.

"Good morning, Mother," he greeted, smiling.

"Sedgewick," she bit out again, looking pale and quite as if she had just learned of a death. "I must speak with you in private at once."

It wasn't like his mother to make demands of him. Mostly because she knew they would be ignored. But he needed to speak with her anyway concerning his plans to wed Joceline, so he allowed it.

Quint inclined his head. "Of course, madam. The drawing room should do."

It was one of the few rooms on this floor in which he hadn't kissed Joceline, and while he intended to fully rectify that matter, it would have to wait until after they were husband and wife. If he wanted to shield her from gossip, he was going to have to keep his desire firmly in check, as impossible a feat as that seemed.

He escorted his mother to the chamber in question, a thorny silence between them, the taut line of her jaw telling him that he was in for a tongue-lashing. When they reached the drawing room, the door had barely closed behind them before she confirmed his suspicion, rounding on him in high dudgeon.

"Sedgewick, I have been beset by the most egregious accusation this morning," she began, "the very scandalous nature of which I can scarcely fathom. It is, without a doubt, the most dreadful, egregious, unbelievable, preposterous outrage I have ever, in all my years on this earth, been forced to confront."

Quint tensed, dread coiling in his stomach. Not from his mother's words, but rather because he feared there was only one thing that would cause such an unprecedented, melodramatic reaction from her.

But he maintained his sangfroid just the same. "I do believe you said egregious twice, Mother."

"It bore repeating. I could have said it thrice." She pressed a bejeweled hand over her heart. "Truly, Sedgewick, I am deeply embarrassed to have to come to you with this, but Lady Diana is positively stricken, and if what she implied is true, then it must be answered for. The poor dear girl was so pale, and she has been weeping uncontrollably all morning."

"I am sorry to hear Lady Diana has been distressed," he said, though, in truth, it hardly concerned him.

He had never harbored any intention of offering for her. He hadn't invited her to Blackwell Abbey. That had all been his mother's manipulations at work.

"As well you should be," his mother said, her voice trembling beneath the force of her upset. "For you are the source of her discontent."

He clenched his jaw and raked a hand through his hair, realizing as he felt the long strands slide against his fingertips that he'd forgotten to don his gloves this morning. "I fail to see how I can be the lady's source of discontent. I have not seen her since last evening at dinner, and I do believe we all parted ways on excellent terms."

His mother's eyes fluttered closed for a moment, as if she were summoning up her strength. She swayed, and he feared she was going to swoon.

"Mother." He caught her elbow in a gentle hold, steadying her as her eyes opened again. "Shall I ring for some hartshorn?"

"No servants, if you please," she clipped, her tone steeped in disapproval. "That is the reason I wished to speak with you, Sedgewick. Lady Diana's lady's maid brought some troubling concerns to her from belowstairs about the nature of your relationship with your *housekeeper*."

Ah, so there it was.

She said the last word as if it were an epithet, and indeed, to Quint, it rather had become one. He disliked thinking of Joceline by that impersonal term. She was so much more to him than a servant. So much more than he could have ever imagined possible.

His gut clenched at the thought that he hadn't been as careful as he'd believed. That he had brought shame and gossip down upon Joceline. But he still didn't know how much anyone knew just yet.

He kept his expression carefully blank. "Oh? And what, pray tell, can be her worry about Mrs. Yorke?"

His mother shuddered. "Her lady's maid suggested that there is a great deal of tongue-wagging among your domestics that you have been improper with the woman. Indeed, Lady Diana's lady's maid said that you were seen belowstairs in the early hours of the morning, and that you were leaving the housekeeper's bedroom. Lady Diana is desperately overset, for she was hoping for a match between the two of you, but no lady can, in good conscience, wed a man who would commit adultery with one of his servants. It is the height of disgrace."

Damn it. He had somehow been seen, and now it was Joceline who would pay the price for his lack of discretion, because he was a duke and she was a domestic—and a woman at that—and that was simply the way of the world.

"I can scarcely believe a young lady of good breeding would carry such a shocking tale to another," he pointed out grimly. "And likewise for her lady's maid."

"I'll own that it was quite irregular," his mother huffed, her eyes flashing with indignant fire. "However, I can hardly find fault with her for trying to make certain that her marriage bed would not be shared by her housekeeper. Tell me it isn't true, Sedgewick, I beg you. Tell me that the lady's maid is engaging in baseless gossip and that she should be sacked at once."

He didn't want to admit it, confound the tongue-wagging lady's maid. He had intended to do things properly. To announce to his mother his intentions to court and marry Joceline. But now, his hand was being forced.

"Mother, I do not now, nor have I ever, harbored any inclination toward marrying Lady Diana," he said instead.

His mother's hand flew over her mouth, stifling a gasp as her eyes went wide. "It's true, then, isn't it?"

He scrubbed at his jaw. "What is true?"

"That you have been indecent with your housekeeper."

"I'll not answer such a question, madam," he denied tersely. "What I will tell you is this. I intend to make Joceline Yorke my wife."

His mother went pale, and this time, she truly did fall backward, nearly collapsing to a heap before he caught her and guided her to a seat.

"You cannot do such a thing," she protested.

"I can, and I will," he said, seating himself nearby, lest she fall out of her chair. "There is nothing you can say to sway me from my course."

"Good God, Sedgewick," she gasped. "Only think of the scandal. Have you gone mad? Of course you must have done. It is the sole explanation for such a ludicrous notion to have entered your head. I knew that no good would come of locking yourself away here at Blackwell Abbey. I warned you of it when you left, did I not? And how many letters have I sent, imploring you to return to civilization? Dozens upon dozens, I'd wager. Instead, you lingered here, allowing your brain to rot."

He might have laughed, were not her accusations so dire.

He gripped the arms of his chair. "Is that what you think, Mother? That I must be mad to wish to marry the woman I love?"

"The woman you *love*? You cannot love her. She's your inferior in every way."

He held his mother's stare, unflinching. "On the contrary, I rather think Mrs. Yorke is my superior in *every* way. And need I remind you that if not for your meddlesome interference, she would not have come to me here at Blackwell Abbey? You sent her to me."

"I sent her to you so that she could gather your house into order, and so that when I brought Lady Diana to you, she would not run screaming back to London. I did not send Mrs. Yorke to you for any reason other than for her to be your housekeeper. Your *servant*. A gentleman does not dally with his domestics. Need I remind you?"

He smiled tightly. "Fortunately for me, Mrs. Yorke will be my duchess. Not my servant."

"But Sedgew—"

The blistering look he gave her stopped her *in medias res*.

"I am marrying her," he repeated firmly. "Not Lady Diana. Not anyone else. I've fallen in love with Mrs. Yorke, and I intend to make her my duchess."

His mother's shoulders stiffened, and her countenance took on a mulish expression he knew too well. "But Lady Diana is perfect for you in every way. She is young and lovely, and she comes from one of the very best families in England."

"How nice for her. I'm still not marrying the chit."

His mother gaped. "And yet you propose to marry this… this…common trollop who has taken you to her bed before all the servants?"

Fury had him shooting to his feet, to the devil with remaining seated in the presence of a lady. At the moment, his mother was certainly not conducting herself like one.

"Apologize for paying her insult," he demanded.

His mother's chin went up. "I'll do no such thing. There is only one sort of woman who would welcome the master of the house into her private quarters when she is nothing more than a servant."

"Yes," he agreed with deceptive calm, "and that is the sort of woman I intend to make my wife. Any lapse in judgment is purely my own. I went to Joceline's room last night uninvited because I couldn't bear to be apart from her a moment longer. I'll not have her paying the price for my own mistakes."

"The fault is mine for this outrage," she said, shaking her head. "I should never have offered her such a tremendous sum to be housekeeper. And then the additional fifty pounds."

His mother's words gave him pause, for he hadn't realized that she had lured Joceline to Durham with a fat purse. "A tremendous sum? How much?"

"One hundred pounds per annum," his mother said, sighing. "I might have known, too, that she was lying about sending every bit of it to her mother and siblings. And then there was the fifty pounds for persuading you to decorate Blackwell Abbey for Christmas. It was meant to be for Lady Diana's sake. I knew she would never agree to become your wife if I brought her to a desolate, decrepit old abbey bereft of any joy."

He ought to have known that her meddling had been greater than merely hiring a housekeeper, and that her actions hadn't been entirely altruistic. But he didn't understand her insistence upon his marrying the earl's daughter.

THE DUKE WHO DESPISED CHRISTMAS

"Why were you hell-bent upon seeing me wed to Lady Diana?" he asked.

A cross expression soured his mother's countenance. "Because I am in love with Lord Dreighton, you ungrateful scoundrel, and he will not marry again until he sees his daughter settled. She suffered a tremendous scandal in London, and all her prospects dried up. I was hoping that Mrs. Yorke would render this heap habitable. It would have been quite ideal, really. Few women will have you with your terrible scars, duke or no, and no gentleman will have Lady Diana, given the gossip. You could have married, and then I could have wed Dreighton as I have been longing to do."

His mother's selfish reasons for wanting to see him married suddenly made perfect, awful sense. None of her plans had been about him. They had all been about herself and her own happiness. To say nothing of the cavalier fashion in which she had referred to his *terrible scars*.

Everything within him went cold. "Mother, I want you, Lady Diana, and the Earl of Dreighton to leave Blackwell Abbey at once, and I never want you to return."

"Leave?" she sputtered. "But it's Christmas Eve."

He didn't care.

"Trains will still be running. They are scheduled for tomorrow as well. I saw the advert in *The Times* myself. I'll have Dunreave make the necessary arrangements."

She rose from her seat, quaking with fury. "Sedgewick, if you force us to leave and insist upon marrying so dreadfully beneath you, I will never forgive you. It is beyond the pale."

He took in his mother, all burning, self-important ire, and he felt oddly at ease. "I don't particularly care, madam. The only good turn you have brought me is sending me Mrs. Yorke. For that, I thank you. Otherwise, I bid you farewell."

With a formal bow, he took his leave.

"I'VE BEEN LOOKING EVERYWHERE for you, Mrs. Yorke."

With a start, Joceline turned from the last bits of holly she had been arranging with some freshly cut orangery flowers on the dining room table. Her heart beat faster as her gaze settled upon Quint on the threshold, looking dapper in country tweed and a notable lack of gloves. He was so handsome, so beloved. It required all the restraint she possessed to keep from running to him and throwing herself into his arms.

Last night had been over in a blink, and she had woken to an empty bed and the fear that what they had shared had been nothing but a feverish dream. Until she had found his neckcloth, partially flung beneath her bed, the only hint that it had been real.

"Your Grace." Remembering herself, she dipped into a curtsy. "I was finishing the table preparation for breakfast this morning."

"That won't be necessary," he said, smiling as he sauntered into the room.

"It won't?" She frowned, confused. "But surely your guests will arrive in a few minutes' time. I wouldn't wish to disappoint them with a barren table."

"My guests are departing this morning," he said, and she couldn't help but to take note of his dimples, making a rare showing. "They'll not be requiring breakfast."

This news was most unexpected.

"But…it's Christmas Eve."

He stopped before her, gazing at her with a look of unfettered tenderness. "So it is."

"Why would they wish to return to London with such short notice, and just before Christmas?" she asked. "Has something not been to their liking? I can have it remedied at once, whatever it is."

"They're returning to London because I told them to go," he said simply. "I've discovered that the only reason they came at all was because Lady Diana requires a husband so that my mother can marry the earl. But Lady Diana was embroiled in some manner of scandal in London, the magnitude of which rendered it more appealing for her to venture to the wilds of the north and consider a hideously scarred recluse as a potential suitor."

She hated the way he spoke of himself, and she also hated the revelation he had just made. "You are not hideously scarred. And I am shocked that Her Grace would so place her own needs before her son's." Belatedly, she realized how forward she was being, recalling the necessary erection of boundaries between them. "Forgive me. I shouldn't have spoken so bluntly."

"You needn't ask for forgiveness." He reached for her, looping his arms around her waist and pulling her flush against him.

"Your Grace," she squeaked in protest, her eyes flying to the closed door, where, at any moment, someone might appear.

"Quint," he said and then kissed her soundly, his mouth hot and devouring.

He felt so wonderful that, for a moment, she forgot why she shouldn't allow him to kiss her in the midst of his dining room just before breakfast. But then she remembered, flattening her palms on his chest and pushing gently.

He lifted his head, still grinning.

And oh, the way he looked—happy. Truly, magnificently, happy.

"You cannot kiss me like this," she whispered. "It's wrong. I'm your housekeeper."

"Not any longer, you're not."

She stiffened, searching his countenance, her brow furrowed. "I don't understand."

"You're sacked," he pronounced with great joy. "You are no longer my housekeeper. Therefore, I am free to kiss you whenever and wherever I like, including in my dining room at half past eight in the morning."

Dread unfurled. "Quint, I need this situation. Please do not give me the sack. My mother and my siblings require everything I send home to them to survive."

"Do you think they would like Blackwell Abbey?" he asked, further confusing her.

She blinked. "Do I think who would like it here? My mother, sisters, and brother?"

"How many of them do you have, by the way?" he asked thoughtfully. "A man likes to prepare."

"Three sisters and one brother," she said. "But I still don't understand. What are you saying?"

His smile faded, his expression turning serious. "I'm saying that you needn't send funds home to your mother and siblings any longer, nor do you have to be a housekeeper. Not ever again. They can come to us here at Blackwell Abbey. There is room aplenty for the five of them."

Her heart iced over. "But I cannot be your mistress, Quint. I'll not do it. Please don't ask it of me."

"My sweet girl, is that what you think of me?" He cupped her cheek, holding her as if she were fashioned of the finest, most delicate porcelain, as if she were priceless to him. "Of course I suppose you must. I've made a muck of this, haven't I?" He stepped away from her suddenly, offering her his hand. "Come with me so I can do this properly, won't you?"

Instinctively, she laced her fingers through his. But then he pulled her from the dining room, taking her into the hall where anyone could see their hands linked.

"Quint," she protested. "Someone will take note."

"Let them." He grinned, tugging her into the library where a cozy fire was roaring and the fresh scent of greenery and fir surrounded them.

It was the scent of Christmas. Of hope.

"But...what are you... This is..." She was breathless, her words trailing away as he stopped beneath the kissing bough she'd had one of the footmen hang from the ceiling.

He turned to her, taking both her hands in his. "I'm not good at pretty phrases, and all my best plans have turned to naught, so I'll just say it. I love you, Joceline Yorke. Not long ago, I believed I would never feel that tender emotion again. I believed myself incapable. In many ways, it was as if I'd died in that fire. But then you barged into my life with Christmas holly and fir trees and a smile that is pure sunshine, and you brought me back to life. Just like the flowers you found in the orangery and coaxed into blossoming again. Marry me. Be my duchess. *Please*."

"Oh, Quint." For a moment, she couldn't find words. Her heart was flooded with so much unimaginable joy that her mind couldn't keep up with itself. She had never believed he would wish to marry her. That he would *love* her. "I love you too. But I'm no duchess. I'm a common girl who has worked in service these last nine years. I don't belong in the gilded world of aristocrats and polite society. I never will. This cannot be what you want."

"Of course it can," he countered tenderly. "And you *do* belong. You belong with me. Say yes, sweet girl. I know I'm too old for you and scarred and—"

"Stop," she interrupted. "You're none of those things. I'll not hear another word of such blasphemy. And yes, I'll marry you. It would be my great honor to be your wife."

The smile he gave her was dazzling. "No, my darling. The honor is all mine."

They kissed beneath the kissing bough as snow began to fall anew, and for the first time since Joceline had been sent away all those years ago, she knew she had finally found her true home.

Right here, in the arms of the man she loved.

EPILOGUE

Just as it had each December for the past ten years, Blackwell Abbey smelled like Christmas. The scent of holly and fir mingled with citrus. Before Quint, the drawing room was decorated with trees, ribbons, candles, kissing boughs, garlands, and all manner of shining trinkets. The fire crackled merrily in the grate. Snow fell beyond the windows, blanketing the earth in a shimmering mantle. Presents were laid out on the table, awaiting the annual tradition of gift-giving that had begun the night he had asked Joceline to marry him. That year, they had given each other their hearts.

But it wasn't the decorations or the traditions this Christmas Eve that filled him with a deep and abiding sense of love and contentedness. It was his family—from nine-year-old Nell, who was a replica of her mother with raven hair and green eyes, to the youngest, two-year-old Robin, who was old enough this year to toddle about and nearly pull down the Christmas trees with his innocent enthusiasm. In between were Clara and Edward, seven and four respectively, and presiding over them all, her belly round with the child that would swell their ranks to one more in early spring, was his beloved wife.

They were joined by her mother, brother, and sisters—one large, exceedingly happy family.

"The eldest gets to give her gift to Papa, and then the second eldest, and so on," Joceline was telling a protesting Edward.

"But I want to be the eldest," Edward said with a pout.

"You can't be the eldest, you silly goose," Nell told her brother. "I'm the eldest, and that means I get to give Papa his present from me first."

She raced for the table in a flurry of skirts, her dark curls bouncing in her exuberance.

"I'm second," Clara announced importantly.

"I don't want to be third," Edward complained.

Robin grasped a handful of Christmas tree and tugged.

Quint scooped his youngest son into his arms. "No pulling down the trees, lad. Mama will be quite cross with you if you do."

"I could never be cross with any of my darlings," Joceline said with the sunny smile that never failed to send desire coursing through him.

Ten years they had been married. Ten glorious, fulfilling, wonderful years. He loved her more with each passing day. They'd caused something of a scandal with their wedding, for it wasn't every day that a duke married his housekeeper. Neither of them had cared, and over time, the gossip had faded. Even his mother had apologized, and although the damage had been done and the two of them remained distant, Quint had forgiven her because Joceline had. His wife's kindhearted, generous nature was one of the qualities he adored about her the most.

But then, there truly wasn't anything about Joceline he didn't adore. She had healed him, shown him how to live again. Shown him how to love again. And she had filled his icy heart with warmth just as she had filled his barren home with laughter and children. It was a second chance he didn't deserve, but one he was damned well glad he'd been given.

Robin patted Quint's cheek, his little fingers sticky. "Papa!"

From the Christmas tree, Quint realized.

Joceline chuckled. "Oh dear, you've covered Papa's face with tree sap."

Nell appeared before him, shyly offering a piece of embroidery. "Here is your gift from me, Papa."

He accepted it, admiring her handiwork. "Such fine work, Nellie. Thank you."

Nell smiled, showing off dimples in both cheeks that were like his own. "It's a Christmas tree."

"So I see." Robin reached for the embroidery with his sticky hand, but Quint held it out of reach. "No sap on my gift, if you please."

"Robin, come to Grandmama," Joceline's mother invited from across the drawing room. "Let your papa receive his presents."

Quint settled a squirming Robin on his feet, grinning as his son raced across the Axminster and clambered onto his grandmother's lap. Clara appeared before him next, another miniature Joceline, but with golden hair.

She offered him a pressed flower picture in a frame. "I made this for you, Papa, and I made another just like it for Grandmama."

"It's lovely," he praised, admiring the way she had painstakingly arranged the dried lily of the valley and iris.

Clara smiled. "Thank you, Papa."

"My turn!" Edward said excitedly, racing forward, something clenched in his small fist.

"And what have we here?" Quint asked, extending his

hand—ungloved, for he had long since stopped covering his scars.

Edward deposited half a gingerbread square in his palm.

"For you, Papa," he declared.

Quint peered down at the offering. "A half-eaten gingerbread. Thank you, son."

"You're welcome, Papa." Edward grinned up at him, a black-haired green-eyed version of himself as a youth. "I know it's your favorite."

"How magnanimous of you, Eddy," Joceline added, biting her lip to keep from laughing.

"I *am* magmanamoose," Edward said proudly, puffing up his chest.

"You're a moose?" Nell teased her younger brother.

"No, I'm maganany-mis," Edward announced.

"Magnanimous," Joceline corrected gently.

"Namganamiss," Edward repeated.

Quint couldn't stifle his own chuckle as he ruffled his son's dark hair affectionately. "It's time for everyone else to receive their presents now. I do hope you haven't eaten your gifts for Grandmama and your cousins."

"I only eated part of yours because I knew you wouldn't mind," his son confided.

Quint shared an amused glance with Joceline. "You may as well eat the rest of it, lad."

Edward's eyes went wide. "May I?"

He nodded. "You may."

His son snatched up the gingerbread and raced across the drawing room to where his grandmother and cousins had begun exchanging presents. Nell and Clara joined them, leaving Quint standing with Joceline, pine sap on his cheek, gingerbread crumbs in his hand, and love in his heart.

"Perhaps next year he won't eat your present," Joceline suggested wryly, resting her hand on her belly's gentle swell.

Quint grinned. "It's rather become our tradition. Last year, it was Christmas cake crumbs."

She laughed. "So it was. I had forgotten. The girls took great pride in making your gifts, but I fear Eddy hasn't the patience for it just yet."

"I already have the greatest gifts anyone could ask for," he told her, staring into her sparkling emerald eyes.

Joceline gave him a look of unabashed tenderness. "As do I, my love."

He reached into his coat, extracted the small box he'd been keeping in an inner pocket, and presented it to her. "Here is one more anyway, sweet girl."

"Quint." She took the box from him. "You needn't have."

He drank in the sight of her, so lovely, so beloved, and thought it impossible to be any happier than he was here and now, in this moment, on Christmas Eve.

"I had every need," he said gently. "Open it."

She lifted the lid, revealing the emerald pendant he'd had commissioned in London for her. "Oh Quint, it's gorgeous."

"Not nearly as gorgeous as you, and the color cannot begin to compare to your eyes, but I suppose it shall do."

"I have a present for you as well," she told him softly, a sultry smile curving her lips, "but I'll give it to you later."

His cock twitched to life at the promise of his gift as he took her into his arms. "I cannot wait for it." He paused and glanced meaningfully up at the decoration hanging above them. "Would you look at that? A kissing bough."

"So it is." Her hands settled on his shoulders, her belly between them as she raised her brows with mock astonishment. "Whatever shall we do?"

"I suppose we'll just have to—"

"Kiss," she interrupted, and then she rose on her toes and pressed her mouth to his there in the drawing room, surrounded by Christmas greenery and everyone they loved.

THANK you so very much for reading *The Duke Who Despised Christmas*! I hope you loved Quint and Joceline's road to happily ever after because I loved every second of writing their story. So begins a new holiday tradition where each year, I'll add a new, stand-alone story to this Christmas series. If you'd like to see what's next from me in the meantime, read on for a small sneak peek of *Duke with a Reputation* (Wicked Dukes Society Book 1), featuring the Duke of Brandon and Lottie, Lady Grenfell, who you may recall meeting in *Her Virtuous Viscount*.

Please stay in touch! The only way to be sure you'll know what's next from me is to sign up for my newsletter here: http://eepurl.com/dyJSar. Please join my reader group for early excerpts, cover reveals, and more here: https://www.facebook.com/groups/scarlettscottreaders. And if you're in the mood to chat all things steamy historical romance and read a different book together each month, join my book club, Dukes Do It Hotter right here: https://www.facebook.com/groups/hotdukes because we're having a whole lot of fun!

Duke with a Reputation
Wicked Dukes Society
Book One

THE DUKE OF BRANDON is London's most infamous rake. But his world crashes to a decided halt when the sins of his past come back to haunt him in the form of one small she-devil of a child who has green eyes just like his. To make matters worse, his disapproving grandmother has decided he must marry or forfeit his inheritance.

Now, he has no choice but to raise a daughter, find a suitable wife, and keep his harridan grandmother from discovering his sordid secrets as the founder of the Wicked Dukes Society. So when the tempting, fiery-haired Countess of Grenfell propositions him, he offers her something else instead—a marriage of convenience.

Lottie, Countess of Grenfell, is London's most notorious widow. Her doomed, one-sided marriage left her with a broken heart and a determination to never wed again. What she wants is simple—passion, independence, and one night in the Duke of Brandon's bed. Or in his scandalous chair. Perhaps even against a wall. She wouldn't marry him, however, if he were the last man on earth.

Brandon is quickly running out of time and his troublemaking daughter has decided no one else shall do as her stepmama but the maddening countess. He must persuade Lottie to become his duchess with all haste or risk losing everything. As he sets out to seduce her into marriage, he's shocked to realize he's done the one thing he previously believed himself incapable of along the way—he's fallen in love. But Lottie's bruised and battered heart is more guarded than his, and she has vowed to never allow another man to hurt her again.

Chapter One

Brandon was having a nightmare.

That was the only explanation for the sight opposite him, he was certain of it. Either that, or he had imbibed one of King's ingenious brews and was now suffering the delusional aftereffects of the dubious elixir.

"Have you nothing to say for yourself, Brandon?"

The sharp, censorious voice, however, was disturbingly real. As was the glacial green-eyed glare so similar to his own. And the massive, billowing silk gown, beneath which hid a crinoline more suited to the fashions of thirty years ago than now.

He blinked, hoping the action would dispel the image before him. Pull him from the throes of sleep. Cast away the demons brought about by one of King's inspired concoctions.

But no.

His grandmother remained.

Hellfire. Perhaps she was real after all.

Brandon cleared his throat. "I do beg your pardon, Grandmother, but I have no notion of what I ought to be saying for myself."

"Have you not heard a word I have just spoken?"

Admittedly, he had been wool-gathering. Hoping he had found himself thrown into some slumberous alternate reality.

"I'm afraid not," he conceded.

Her nostrils flared, and for a fanciful moment, he imagined her breathing fire like a mythical dragon swooping in to scorch him and other unsuspecting mortals in her path.

"I will begin again, Brandon," she said succinctly, as if she feared very much he possessed the mental acuity to comprehend. "Do try to heed me this time."

Her scolding was nothing new; Grandmother had always been harder than granite. Although her dark hair had long since turned snowy and the face that had made her the most-sought-after debutante of her day was now lined, there was nary a hint of infirmity surrounding her. She was a tiny wren of a woman, but sturdy of form.

Now, as ever, she terrified him.

Brandon shifted on his dashed uncomfortable chair,

wishing he'd had the forethought to have Grandmother await him somewhere other than the drawing room, a chamber he scarcely used for its Louis Quinze devotion. "Of course. Pray, proceed."

She inclined her head and with a regal air, continued. "As I was saying, a visitor most unexpected and uninvited paid a call upon me yesterday. I am told she was turned away by your domestics. Ordinarily, I would have no desire to concern myself with such matters. Indeed, it is most unseemly. However, the child has your eyes and nose."

Surely he must have misheard.

"The child?" he repeated, feeling as if the world had suddenly turned on its head.

Everything before him was unrecognizable.

"The girl child," Grandmother elaborated, disapproval dripping from her voice.

Brandon was still struggling to understand. Was there wine about? A cursory glance of the drawing room suggested only tea that Grandmother must have requested. He needed something far less tepid.

"Are you attending me, Brandon?" she asked, her voice sharp.

He wrested his gaze from the tea and pinned it back upon his grandmother. "What girl child?"

"The one who was delivered, much to my butler's horror, to my door yesterday afternoon by her mother, just before the woman ran off with her lover."

"Who was the girl's mother?" he managed, his necktie feeling more like a noose by the moment, growing tighter and tighter.

"She said her name was Mrs. Helena Darby-Booth." Grandmother's lip curled as if she had just tasted something spoiled. "A woman of ill repute, to be sure. She was dressed like a harlot, and it is to my everlasting shame that such a sinful creature should have had cause to arrive at my door after having been refused from yours. Have you any notion of the tongues that will gleefully wag? No, I dare say you do not. You are too busy cavorting with your lemans to save a thought for anyone other than yourself. Just like your father. I warned my darling Diana not to wed that scurrilous scoundrel. I didn't care that he was a duke."

His grandmother shook her head, caught in the throes of the past and temporarily distracted from her diatribe. Brandon was in shock. Helena had been his lover off and on over the years until she had abruptly married and left the stage some time ago. Had not that man been called Booth? Brandon searched the dim recesses of his mind for the name and the particulars. He had not seen her since, and nor had he heard from her. What cause had she to call upon his grandmother, bringing a girl child?

One with his eyes and nose?

He swallowed against a rising sea of bile. "The sins of the father, madam. Tell me, if you please, why Mrs. Darby-Booth should have called upon you, bringing a child."

"Because Mrs. Darby-Booth is following her new gentleman friend to America, and according to the letter she left with the girl, the man in question could only afford passage for two." His grandmother's green eyes, assessing and bright, narrowed. "She was required to leave the child behind, and she therefore deemed it better to leave the child in the care of her father's family rather than an orphanage."

No, no, no. He heard the words Grandmother was speaking, but he didn't wish to understand them. Surely this was all a dreadful mistake. Some manner of ploy Helena had concocted. He had always taken care with his mistresses. He used a sheath. Unless…there had been occasions, particularly in times of drunken revelry at Wingfield Hall or in St John's Wood when he may have been too sotted to take care…

Dread seized him, a fist choking his lungs.

"In the care of her…father's family?" he repeated.

"Yes, since the father himself refused to see her. There was a ship leaving, and our Mrs. Darby-Booth only had so much time in which to complete the task of abandoning her bastard child."

His grandmother was forbidding.

Bastard child.

The father.

Eyes and nose like his.

A daughter.

Want more? Get *Duke with a Reputation* now!

DON'T MISS SCARLETT'S OTHER ROMANCES!

Complete Book List
HISTORICAL ROMANCE

Heart's Temptation
A Mad Passion (Book One)
Rebel Love (Book Two)
Reckless Need (Book Three)
Sweet Scandal (Book Four)
Restless Rake (Book Five)
Darling Duke (Book Six)
The Night Before Scandal (Book Seven)

Wicked Husbands
Her Errant Earl (Book One)
Her Lovestruck Lord (Book Two)
Her Reformed Rake (Book Three)
Her Deceptive Duke (Book Four)
Her Missing Marquess (Book Five)
Her Virtuous Viscount (Book Six)

DON'T MISS SCARLETT'S OTHER ROMANCES!

Wicked Dukes Society
Duke with a Reputation (Book One)

Christmas Dukes
The Duke Who Despised Christmas (Book One)

League of Dukes
Nobody's Duke (Book One)
Heartless Duke (Book Two)
Dangerous Duke (Book Three)
Shameless Duke (Book Four)
Scandalous Duke (Book Five)
Fearless Duke (Book Six)

Notorious Ladies of London
Lady Ruthless (Book One)
Lady Wallflower (Book Two)
Lady Reckless (Book Three)
Lady Wicked (Book Four)
Lady Lawless (Book Five)
Lady Brazen (Book 6)

Unexpected Lords
The Detective Duke (Book One)
The Playboy Peer (Book Two)
The Millionaire Marquess (Book Three)
The Goodbye Governess (Book Four)

Dukes Most Wanted
Forever Her Duke (Book One)
Forever Her Marquess (Book Two)
Forever Her Rake (Book Three)
Forever Her Earl (Book Four)
Forever Her Viscount (Book Five)

DON'T MISS SCARLETT'S OTHER ROMANCES!

Forever Her Scot (Book Six)

The Wicked Winters
Wicked in Winter (Book One)
Wedded in Winter (Book Two)
Wanton in Winter (Book Three)
Wishes in Winter (Book 3.5)
Willful in Winter (Book Four)
Wagered in Winter (Book Five)
Wild in Winter (Book Six)
Wooed in Winter (Book Seven)
Winter's Wallflower (Book Eight)
Winter's Woman (Book Nine)
Winter's Whispers (Book Ten)
Winter's Waltz (Book Eleven)
Winter's Widow (Book Twelve)
Winter's Warrior (Book Thirteen)
A Merry Wicked Winter (Book Fourteen)

The Sinful Suttons
Sutton's Spinster (Book One)
Sutton's Sins (Book Two)
Sutton's Surrender (Book Three)
Sutton's Seduction (Book Four)
Sutton's Scoundrel (Book Five)
Sutton's Scandal (Book Six)
Sutton's Secrets (Book Seven)

Rogue's Guild
Her Ruthless Duke (Book One)
Her Dangerous Beast (Book Two)
Her Wicked Rogue (Book 3)

Royals and Renegades

DON'T MISS SCARLETT'S OTHER ROMANCES!

How to Love a Dangerous Rogue (Book One)
How to Tame a Dissolute Prince (Book Two)

Sins and Scoundrels
Duke of Depravity
Prince of Persuasion
Marquess of Mayhem
Sarah
Earl of Every Sin
Duke of Debauchery
Viscount of Villainy

Sins and Scoundrels Box Set Collections
Volume 1
Volume 2

The Wicked Winters Box Set Collections
Collection 1
Collection 2
Collection 3
Collection 4

Wicked Husbands Box Set Collections
Volume 1
Volume 2

Notorious Ladies of London Box Set Collections
Volume 1

The Sinful Suttons Box Set Collections
Volume 1

Stand-alone Novella
Lord of Pirates

DON'T MISS SCARLETT'S OTHER ROMANCES!

CONTEMPORARY ROMANCE
Love's Second Chance
Reprieve (Book One)
Perfect Persuasion (Book Two)
Win My Love (Book Three)

Coastal Heat
Loved Up (Book One)

ABOUT THE AUTHOR

USA Today and Amazon bestselling author Scarlett Scott writes steamy Victorian and Regency romance with strong, intelligent heroines and sexy alpha heroes. She lives in Pennsylvania and Maryland with her Canadian husband, their adorable identical twins, a demanding diva of a dog, and one zany cat who showed up one summer and never left.

A self-professed literary junkie and nerd, she loves reading anything, but especially romance novels and poetry. Catch up with her on her website https://scarlettscottauthor.com. Hearing from readers never fails to make her day.

Scarlett's complete book list and information about upcoming releases can be found at https://scarlettscottau thor.com.

Connect with Scarlett! You can find her here:
   Join Scarlett Scott's reader group on Facebook for early excerpts, giveaways, and a whole lot of fun!
   Sign up for her newsletter here
   https://www.tiktok.com/@authorscarlettscott

- facebook.com/AuthorScarlettScott
- x.com/scarscoromance
- instagram.com/scarlettscottauthor
- bookbub.com/authors/scarlett-scott
- amazon.com/Scarlett-Scott/e/B004NW8N2I
- pinterest.com/scarlettscott

Printed in Great Britain
by Amazon